The Drifter

RED RIDGE CHRONICLES BOOK 2

SARAH LAMB

A thank you to my proofreader, Brooke, and all of the lovely women who help ARC read to catch those typos I miss!

This book was not written by AI. Any typos are proudly (and embarrassingly!) my own human created ones!

This book is not allowed to be used in training AI.

Paperback ISBN: 978-1-960418-37-1
Large print ISBN: 978-1-960418-38-8

Contents

To each of the special people who have helped me bring this series and many of my other books to life: Brooke, for her on-point suggestions and proofreading; Nancy, for her fantastic covers; Spencer, for his incredible narration; and you, dear readers, for your endless support.

Chapter 1

1880s, Red Ridge, Oregon

A violin, low and mournful, traveled over the yard. Billy Madison closed his eyes and, for just a moment, let the smile he usually wore slip. Somehow, Gavin's music spoke to his soul in a way that he didn't like. That reminded him he was alone. Empty inside.

It wasn't completely true. He knew that. Billy wasn't alone in the sense that he was by himself. After all, Gavin was nearby. Down a way, across the large pasture, Eli and Hannah were likely tucking their children into bed, and Old Gus was probably chewing on a licorice and frowning over the newspaper he enjoyed getting each Tuesday.

So, no, not alone in a physical sense. Or even one of friendship. But more in the way of how he knew he was missing half his soul.

Billy looked over at Gavin. "Think we're going to find women too?" he asked suddenly.

Without stopping the bow strokes, Gavin asked, "What has you worried about that? We've never been ones to even consider settling down. That's why it was such a surprise Eli answered that ad to help out Hannah and then fell in love."

"I know it." Billy nodded. "But for some reason, seeing them happy together makes me think about my parents and how happy they are together."

"I see." Gavin continued to play, his tone that of only half paying attention. Billy thought his friend had stopped the conversation when Gavin asked, "And just who is it who has your attention?"

Billy grinned. He couldn't help it. Each time he thought about her, his lips and cheeks moved of their own accord. It was a large, silly, strange smile that about threatened to crack his face in half. "Mirabelle Blackstone," he answered.

There was a screech of the violin, and the music stopped. "The pastor's daughter?" Gavin asked, his voice filled with disbelief.

Billy shrugged.

"The pastor's daughter." Gavin shook his head. "Billy, you know her pa will never agree. You and me...we aren't respectable folk. You know that. We're gunslingers."

"We're lawmen," Billy protested, though it was true not everyone felt the same. "Guns for hire. And we take the jobs that help, not hurt."

"Be that as it may," Gavin said, and pointed the bow at Billy, "I can't see Pastor Blackstone wanting his only child—a daughter, no less—married to a gunslinger. Not with the reputations we have."

Billy chewed on the end of a stick of jerky. Gavin wasn't wrong. Every word he said was true. Pastor Blackstone wouldn't like it. Oh, he preached forgiveness. Love and charity. Doing unto others. But he was still wary of them after they'd moved into town and bought land.

It didn't matter that they'd stopped the crooked sheriff, saved Hannah's home and her life, as well as that of her children. Billy Madison, Gavin Jefferson, and the third of their group, Eli Jones, were notorious gunslingers. It might not have even mattered that they'd done nothing but good for the town and its folks since they moved in.

What mattered to the pastor was his daughter. Billy reckoned it was understandable, and chances were if he had a daughter, he'd be just the same. However, Mirabelle had caught his eye, set his heart thumping, and his mind spinning.

Billy leaned back in his chair as Gavin started playing again. "Well then," he said, kicking his feet up onto the railing. "I reckon I'd better figure out how to change his mind."

Chapter 2

"You'll never change your father's mind," Mrs. Blackstone said as she shook her head at Mirabelle. "I don't care what others are doing. That dress is a half inch too short."

"But, Mama," Mirabelle said, "my boots more than cover my ankles. There's not a bit of skin showing."

Her mother raised an eyebrow and fixed Mirabelle with a look that would brook no disagreement. "Are you arguing with me?"

"No, Mama," Mirabelle said, lowering her head.

At twenty-two, wasn't she old enough to choose her dress length? It would be so nice to be able to walk down the sidewalks in town without sweeping them with her hem!

The seamstress lowered the hem and pinned it, then looked at her mother. "Is this better?"

Mrs. Blackstone peered at it critically, then nodded. "Yes. Much better. Thank you. Now you'll be respectable-looking when you attend Callie's party."

Mirabelle pressed her lips together and held as still as she could while the seamstress pinned around the bottom of the dress. She'd rather wear it than not, even if it was a longer hem than she liked. A half inch might not seem like much, but it was. Sometimes, that small length made stairs difficult to navigate, especially when it was unseemly to raise one's skirts much to walk.

Her dearest friend, Callie, had actually sprained her ankle recently when she'd been stepping down the general store's single step and caught the toe of her boot on her hem. It was lucky her ankle hadn't broken.

Mirabelle tried to ignore the injustice of it all, instead focusing on the full-length mirror before her. The dress, a light spring green, perfectly suited her. Her dark hair was braided into a bun, and she was sure, if she wanted, she'd be able to catch the eye of any young man at the birthday party she'd been invited to. It was just good timing that her mother had agreed she could have a new dress. She'd be able to wear it there.

With poor Callie still unable to do much, she'd need her friends there to cheer her up. It wasn't every day one turned twenty-two. She would be married soon, of that Mirabelle was sure. Callie had many beaus, but had gotten quite serious about one in particular. Mirabelle, however, was not in a rush. She'd know the man when she saw him. And she'd not yet spotted him.

"I'll get these alterations done and the dress returned to you this week," the seamstress said, and stepped back once she'd completed her pinning. "Do you need help out of the dress?"

"No, I can manage, thank you," Mirabelle said, and moved behind the folding screen of the shop. A moment later, she'd wriggled out of the dress, pleased she'd not gotten a single poke from the pins.

As she and her mother left the shop and walked onto the sidewalk, Mirabelle sighed.

"What's wrong, dear?" her mother asked. "I thought you loved that dress. Don't tell me that a half inch in length really has you so distressed."

"It's not that," Mirabelle said.

She walked in silence, wanting to ask her mother the question that had burned within her so much as of late, but she wasn't sure she should. She'd been raised not to question the things her parents did. As the daughter of a pastor, it wasn't seemly. Her whole life—one of service, sacrifice, and sweet behavior—had been laid out for her since birth.

"You can tell me if there's a problem," her mother said. "We can turn around and change the pleats if you'd like."

"It's not that," Mirabelle said. "It's not the dress at all, Mama. I love the dress, even if I would prefer it raised slightly so I didn't trip. There's just something else that's been bothering me."

"What is it?"

Mirabelle bit her lip. Their home, a modest yet comfortable two story, was only a few moments' walk away. If she wanted to be sure her father wouldn't overhear her, she needed to ask now.

Summoning her courage, Mirabelle paused and faced her mother, who had also stopped. "It's Papa," she said. "Why does he always get the final say? Women should have a say, especially over the things that concern them. In fact, many do. And rights in other things. Why don't we? I see how Papa orders you about. You always are helping others without any time to rest."

"I enjoy serving," her mother said mildly.

"It's not just the serving," Mirabelle protested. "It's the rules. What you must wear, what you must serve at a tea. It's...stifling. And..." She shook her head, at a loss for words. Finally, one came. "It's unfair."

"Perhaps it seems that way at times," her mother said, wrapping her arm in Mirabelle's. "However, your father has always taken good care of us. He does what he thinks is best."

"Exactly. What *he* thinks is best."

Her mother continued as though she hadn't spoken, "We should respect that and trust him. After all, he has a position and a reputation in this town he must uphold. As part of his family, we must do the same."

Mirabelle didn't answer. She was trying too hard not to roll her eyes.

"Look out!"

The shout caused Mirabelle to startle away from the shop window she'd been peering into. A runaway wagon was rushing down the street. Worse, a woman was standing in the middle of the street, frozen in fear. She started to move, but it would be too late.

Out of nowhere, a man rushed across to her and pulled the woman to safety. She was instantly surrounded by the townspeople. Mirabelle realized she was stuck to the spot as well. In just the blink of an eye, things could have been very different.

"That man had no thought for himself," she said in wonder.

She watched as he bade the woman goodbye, then crossed to their side of the street. "Ladies," he said, tipping his hat.

"That was marvelous of you," Mirabelle said, slightly shocked she dared to address him. She'd seen the man here and there in town, but had never spoken to him before. What had possessed her to do so now?

"It was part luck," he said, giving her a grin. "I happened to be in the right place at the right time."

"Billy!"

The man, Billy, she now assumed, turned away and raised his hand. "On my way, Gus." He tipped his hat again, and hurried over toward an old man in front of the general store.

Mirabelle watched him leave. A very strange feeling formed in her. She felt warm, and tickly and lightheaded all at once and throughout her entire body. She hardly noticed as her mother pulled her back down the sidewalk.

Her heart started to pound, and a slow smile formed.

I think I've just spotted my man.

Chapter 3

Billy jogged over to Gus. "We ready?" he asked. He was helping the old ranch hand to get the wagon loaded up for Hannah. Gus had driven her into town to get supplies, while Eli, his close friend, was checking out a few new horses for sale.

"Just need to get the rest from the store," Gus said. He rubbed one hand against his lower back, then added, "It's not that I can't do it, of course. But Hannah told me to get you. Don't want to make her mad. She's making cherry pie tonight. Want to make sure I get seconds."

Billy laughed. "Of course," he agreed.

Hannah wouldn't withhold anything from Gus. That was the man's way of trying to save face. He had no idea how old Gus was, but he knew he was far too old to be lifting heavy sacks. The man had more than earned the right to rest, especially after he'd taken care of Hannah and her daughter, and arranged for the gunslingers to come and save her home.

Gus was family now, and Billy was fond of the old man. He enjoyed telling him stories—and listening to them in return. Gus might be slowing down a little, but his mind was sharp as a tack, and Billy found him good to converse with.

Whistling, Billy pushed open the general store door. Hannah stood at the counter, looking at a catalog. He walked up to her. "Afternoon, Hannah."

She smiled up at him. "Thank you for helping us. I'm not sure how much longer Eli will be, and Gus said his knee is hurting."

"Bad storm on the way?" Billy chuckled.

"You laugh, young feller," Gus grumbled as he opened the door. "But one day, you'll understand."

Billy pointed to his right elbow. "I feel it sometimes here," he said solemnly. "Just a twinge now and again, but I do."

Gus nodded in satisfaction. "See?" He squinted and peered at the jars of penny candy. "Let me get a quarter's worth," he said. "Mix it up."

The shopkeeper, Mrs. Stover, nodded and prepared a bag.

Billy picked up a large sack of flour and carried it out to the wagon. His eyes trailed up the street to where he'd seen the preacher's daughter. He'd seen her around town several times and always was looking for her. Today, however, was the first time he'd spoken to her.

A voice like an angel, that's how he'd describe it. She was beautiful, but that wasn't why she made him interested in her. She had a good head on her shoulders. Not once had he seen her giggling or gossiping. In fact, there had been a fire a few months back at one of the buildings in town. Mirabelle had rolled up her sleeves and pitched in with the rest of the townsfolk helping to clean and rebuild. He admired that. It was obvious she wasn't afraid of work, and that she also had the desire to help others.

He recognized a little bit of himself in her. Maybe that's why she called to him.

"Are you okay?"

Billy startled. When had Hannah walked up to him? He grunted, "Yes, just was lost in thought."

"About what?" Eli clapped him on the back.

With a shrug, Billy grinned. "Mirabelle Blackstone."

"Have you said hello to her?" Hannah asked.

"Not...exactly," Billy admitted. "I want to. It's just, I know I can't have a girl like that."

"Why not?" Eli asked. "She not good enough for you?"

"Oh, she's good enough," Billy said, then realized he'd sighed. Likely sounded like a lovesick fool. "No, it's her pa. You know."

They all nodded. Hannah rested her hand on his arm. "You've been here for a while now, Billy, and helped the town many times. Yes, you are a gunslinger. That's something you'll always be, but you are a lot more too. Why, if the pastor can't see past that and accept you to court his daughter, we'll have to convince him otherwise."

Billy laughed and pushed his hat up on his head. "I can look after myself," he said, winking at her. "Besides, who was talking about courting?"

"You were. Night before last at supper." Eli grinned.

Pretty sure his face was on fire, Billy just grunted and pushed at a box in the back of the wagon. "I'll think on it," he promised. "Maybe I will ask her pa. Worst he can do is say no."

"There are a good number of women who'd be interested in you," Hannah said. "Though I know none have caught your eye like Mirabelle has."

"It's true," Billy said. "None have. There's something special about her. It's…" He looked at Eli, and then Hannah. "How did you know? About each other?"

He didn't let himself feel ashamed for asking. Eli had been through a lot with him, and Hannah was now like his older sister. Whatever they told him, he'd listen to carefully. He wanted what they had. Real love. Something that no one could deny when they saw the two of them together.

Hannah's cheeks were pink, and she said softly, "It just happened. Something in me knew."

With a nod, Eli agreed. "That's right. Just knew there'd be a hole in my heart without her." He looked at Hannah fondly. "Still would be."

Billy walked a few steps away. He didn't want to interrupt their moment. It also made a pang form in his heart at the lack of such a thing in his own life.

Once again, his eyes traveled down the street until they landed on the church. Was that how it was? You just...knew? Because he'd been feeling it for a long time.

"What do you suggest I do?" he asked, turning and facing his friends. "How can I stand a better chance with her pa?"

Chapter 4

It was all Mirabelle could do not to gape. The long table set up against the side wall of Callie's mother's living room was filled to bursting with pastries both sweet and savory, delicate finger foods, miniature desserts, and punch, lemonade, and mint tea. Mirabelle had never seen such an extravagant display before.

Daughter to a wealthy businessman, Callie was Mirabelle's dearest friend. Most of the time. Being so wealthy made it hard for her friend to always understand that not everyone lived in such luxury—especially here in the West. It wasn't that Callie ever meant to be snooty. She was just sheltered and spoiled. Things Mirabelle had no experience with, but occasionally wished she did.

"Mirabelle! You've arrived!" Callie stood up and limped over, embracing her. "I'm so glad you are here."

"Thank you for inviting me," Mirabelle said, and offered the small parcel she'd brought.

"You didn't have to bring me anything! But thank you," Callie said with a smile. "May I open it now? And of course I invited you. You are my dearest friend." She laughed then. "It is a fortunate thing for me, as I know I can't always be easy to get along with."

"I won't answer that," Mirabelle teased. "But yes, you may open it."

She watched a little anxiously as Callie carefully untied the ribbon around the small white parcel. Would her friend, so used to having whatever she wanted, be disappointed with such a simple gift? She hoped not. No matter Callie was always delighted, she still had this same worry each birthday and Christmas celebration that passed.

The paper fell away, and Callie gasped. "Oh! What a dear little book. Thank you!"

As she wrapped her arms around Mirabelle again, Mirabelle couldn't help but feel a little relieved. The book, a journal really, wasn't very large, about palm-sized, perhaps a little bigger, but she knew how much Callie enjoyed writing, and hoped she'd make use of it.

"I know just how I shall use it," Callie said. "I've been thinking of a story I'd like to write."

"Will you let me read it once you have finished?" Mirabelle asked.

"Of course!" Callie answered. Then she gestured to the food. "Please, help yourself. Everyone is just mingling. Because of my ankle, I've plopped myself here, near the door. I can talk to everyone who enters, but also not have to move far."

Mirabelle let her gaze float around the room for a moment. There were at least a dozen young women in the room. They stood in small clusters, chattering and eating. Mirabelle frowned. "You are all by yourself," she said, almost scolding. "And here it is, your party."

Callie shrugged. "Many wanted to be invited. That doesn't mean it was because of me."

Pressing her lips together, Mirabelle squeezed her friend's arm. "Not everyone appreciates true friendship," she said. "Some simply like appearances."

Her friend nodded, but Mirabelle didn't miss the sad look.

"Let me bring you a plate," Mirabelle said, and hurried away before Callie could object. In a few moments she'd returned with two plates heaping with finger foods. As she nibbled on a sausage wrapped in pastry, she her mind drifted suddenly to the man she'd seen a few days before.

Billy.

She must have smiled at the memory, because Callie gasped and poked her in the arm. "You've met a man," she said.

Mirabelle startled. "I have not," she disagreed.

But a slow smile spread across her friend's face, and as it did, Mirabelle felt her cheeks burn. "You did. I can tell." Callie leaned closer. "Who is he?"

"I don't know," Mirabelle confessed. She dropped her voice. "I didn't meet him. Not really. I witnessed him save a woman when a runaway wagon headed her way. Something about him...I can't explain it, Callie. But it drew me toward him. I do hope I get to see him again."

"Do you know his name?" her friend asked.

"Billy. That's all I know." Mirabelle shrugged, and stood to retrieve two glasses of punch. As she handed Callie hers, she noticed her wide eyes.

"Do you know him?" Mirabelle asked.

"Know of him, only," Callie said. "Billy Madison. That's his full name." Then she whispered, "He's a gunslinger."

The word sent shivers through Mirabelle. A gunslinger? Now she knew why Callie was so surprised. She felt that way too. He hadn't appeared at all what she thought a gunslinger might. Weren't gunslingers uncouth, dirty, hard around the eyes, and evil?

A small flash of disappointment filled her. Why was it the one man she'd ever seen who interested her had to be a gunslinger? There was no way her parents would even let her close to such a man.

"Have you seen his friends?" Callie giggled. "They're so handsome too. Mama tells me to keep away for my reputation, even though Papa says they are good men."

"Are they?" Mirabelle asked.

"Mm-hmm. You know Hannah Carson? Well, I guess she's not a Carson anymore, after marrying that one gunslinger. He saved her home and protected her when her evil brother-in-law was trying to force her to marry him." Callie's eyes were wide at the retelling. "It's such a romantic story. Perhaps I'll write it in my new book!"

"I think I remember hearing something about that," Mirabelle mused. She took a bite of a lemon cookie. "Didn't it turn out the sheriff was crooked too?"

"That's right," Callie said. "And that's why we don't have a sheriff right now." She bit her lip. "Papa sure wishes we did. I do too. It makes me nervous with as many folks as we get coming to town now, and no real protection."

Mirabelle thought about that. She supposed, as daughter to a pastor, she'd never had to worry about her family being hurt or her family getting robbed. They weren't as well off as some. The small house they lived in didn't have luxury items, only those of a serviceable nature.

"Still," Callie continued, "Papa says he's not worried about it. That if we needed help, now that those gunslingers have made our town their home, we'll all be safe."

"I suppose that's true," Mirabelle murmured, and raised her punch to her lips. She then smiled over the rim of her glass at Callie. "With all you've told me, I wonder if I might stand a chance to get to know him a little better."

Chapter 5

Billy set his napkin on the table, pulled out some money, and handed it to the young woman who had been serving him at lunch.

"Thank you," she said with a smile as he walked out.

He nodded, jammed his hands into his pant pockets, and strolled out into the sunshine. It was a beautiful day, and his belly was filled with beef stew and flaky hot biscuits. The sun was bright, warm, and the air clean and filled with promise. There was just one thing missing, Billy thought as he passed couple after couple. He also wanted a woman on his arm.

"Mr. Madison!"

Billy turned at his name and saw the shopkeeper of a small store waving at him.

"Hello!" he answered. "How can I help?"

"Are you passing by the church, perhaps?" the man asked. "My delivery boy isn't back yet, and Pastor Blackstone asked for an urgent delivery of paper and ink for his sermons."

"I'm happy to take it," Billy said. He felt pleased he'd stopped. This good deed could work in his favor.

"I'd be obliged," the shopkeeper said, then vanished. A moment later, he returned with a small parcel, which Billy accepted.

He tried to keep the eagerness from his step as he walked down the sidewalk and to the small church. Would Mirabelle be inside the church too? He sure hoped so. Then he could say hello. See her beautiful face. The idea made his pulse jump a little.

Regardless of her presence or lack thereof, this would be his chance to talk to the pastor, perhaps get the man to see he wasn't some ruffian or rogue. That he was a good, honest, hardworking man. Just the sort of fellow the pastor wanted for his daughter.

Stepping through the doors of the church, Billy looked around. He wasn't quite sure where the pastor might be. Admittedly, he didn't join in on Sunday services as much as he probably ought to. Maybe that should change.

Clearing this throat, he tried to make his presence known. A moment later, footsteps, slow and measured on the maple floorboards, reached him, coming from a small door in the front.

"Mr. Madison," Pastor Blackstone said, stopping at one of the wooden pews. "What a surprise."

Billy offered the bundle. "I was asked to bring your paper and ink since I was passing by."

"Oh." The pastor looked down at the package. There was a strange hesitation on his face, and he forced out, "Thank you."

"You're welcome." Billy hitched his thumbs into his belt. His heart was hammering, and he was trying to get it to calm so he could focus. Ask his question to the pastor.

He didn't understand why he was feeling jittery. Why, that one time in Mexico, he'd taken on four men. In Colorado, there was that guy twice as big as him, slippery as a snake, and with a deadly gang all reaching for their guns. He hadn't flinched once when he'd ducked and dodged, spun and tackled, laying out justice to each of them. But for some reason, standing in front of the pastor was making his knees feel like knocking.

It wasn't because this was a house of God, Billy mused. No, it was because this was Mirabelle's father. And he wanted to get to know her better.

Billy sighed to himself. There was nothing for it but to ask. What kind of man was he, if he was letting that get in his way of potential happiness?

"You look like you've something on your mind," the pastor said, giving him an opening.

"I do, actually," Billy said. "I'd like to ask you a question."

"Such as?" The pastor raised a brow. Billy almost envied him. He couldn't do just one. They both rose at the same time.

"I wanted permission to call sometime on your daughter."

There was a loud thud as Pastor Blackstone dropped his package. "My...my daughter," he repeated. "Mirabelle."

"That's her, all right," Billy said. He stooped over and retrieved the bundle, handing it over. "Unless you've got another I didn't know about."

Pastor Blackstone stiffened, and Billy realized it was a good thing he hadn't added more to his joke. The first part hadn't gone over very well.

"I do not," the pastor said. He was clutching the package to his chest as though it were a shield. "However, I didn't realize the two of you were acquainted."

"We're not. Not too much, anyway," Billy said. "I'd like to change that. I can tell she's a special woman, and I'd like to spend time with her."

Pastor Blackstone pressed his lips together and shook his head. "I'm sorry. No. There are other young ladies if you are looking to settle. I've got nothing against you, but I want something else for my daughter."

"Something else?" Billy fought to keep the sneer out of his voice. "Like what?"

The pastor stammered. "Yes. To be blunt, someone respectable. Not a man who might have made his money dubiously. As you say yourself, Mirabelle is special, and I want to keep her and her reputation intact."

Billy's jaw clenched. His hands curled into fists before he realized he'd done it. Taking in a slow breath, he relaxed them, then spoke calmly, even though every inch of his being wanted to be anything but.

"I assure you, neither you nor your daughter have anything to fear from me in regards to reputation. Everything I've done, my entire life, has been lawful. Each dollar in my account, and I've plenty of them I assure you, was for catching the criminals and the worst of the humans this world has, and putting them away so they wouldn't harm people like you or your daughter."

Hurt might have carried through on his words. Billy didn't know. He also didn't care. He was too stunned and too upset. His whole life, he'd done the hard things, the right things. *Should have known that even this, there wouldn't be a reward for.*

The pastor looked like he was going to say something, but he closed his mouth. When silence filled the chapel to a point that was almost suffocating, Billy shook his head. There was nothing more to say. Not right now. As a gunslinger, he knew this. You learned when to show your strength, when to restrain it. There were many times that it wouldn't make a lick of difference for the good of something, only make things worse if you kept going. He sensed this was one of those times.

"Good day, Pastor," Billy answered instead, and turned, exiting the church.

A mixture of hurt and anger filled him, and the tight pressure in his chest made it hard to breathe. Yes. The gunslinger in him knew this wasn't the time to battle, but the man inside of him was torn, wanting to lash out for the woman he was attracted to.

As though he hadn't a care in the world, Billy whistled as he walked. Some little ditty he'd picked up in a bar in Arizona. It was catchy. Don't let on if you're rattled. That was something he'd learned a long time ago.

Though he looked calm, his mind was anything but. That didn't matter, though, to Billy Madison. He was determined to show the pastor he wasn't just a gunslinger, but a man in love too.

Chapter 6

Mirabelle's lower lip trembled. She wasn't sure if it was from hurt or shock or anger. The soapy dish in her hands threatened to slip and break, so she carefully placed it down and took a deep breath.

"My word," her mother gasped. "Get to know our Mirabelle better?"

"That's right," her father said, his tone grim. "But like I just told you, I said no."

Mirabelle swallowed past the tightness in her throat. She was trying very hard to keep her temper, to not say something that might get her in trouble or upset her parents. "May I ask why?" she finally settled on. "Am I not allowed any say in the men who wish to know me better? After all, this should be something I do have an opinion on."

Her mother looked at her with a mix of horror and sorrow. "My dear! You can't mean you feel so desperate you'd entertain the thought of a *gunslinger* courting you?"

"He's a good man," Mirabelle said firmly. "I sense it, and everyone else says so. While I don't know if I would want to court or not, I'd at least like to have the opportunity to learn more about if he's someone for me or not."

"Everyone else says so?" her mother sputtered. "If everyone else said the sky was green, would you say that as well?" She looked at her husband. "Such ridiculousness."

Mirabelle had hoped her parents would respond differently, though she knew that had been a false hope. Her father was shaking his head. She knew that look. No one argued with her father. Whether it was simply because he was the man of the house or a pastor, she wasn't sure. Her mother had never, not to Mirabelle's knowledge, contradicted her father. It was something that both infuriated and disappointed her. He was a good man. Of that, she had no doubt at all. But sometimes, he forgot that she wasn't a little girl. That she could—and should—make decisions for herself.

"I know that men can change," her father started in a lecturing tone. "The Bible is full of stories of that. Think of Jonah. Paul. There are others as well. However, I also know that a man—or woman—can be led astray easily, and what may appear as a sheep is actually a wolf in disguise."

Mirabelle's mother was nodding along, her head bobbing. Would it topple off one day, Mirabelle wondered, with as rapidly as it was moving?

"I highly doubt that Mr. Madison is a wolf in sheep's clothing," Mirabelle said with a frown.

"He might not be," her father agreed. "I know the man has done a lot of good in town. I'm not saying he hasn't. He's helped a great number of folks. So have his friends. But the fact remains that you are my daughter, and I want what's best for you."

"I understand, Papa," Mirabelle said, looking at the worn rug beneath her boots.

"Since those gunslingers moved to town, oddly, I've never been concerned about them at all. What I am concerned about is your reputation," he continued.

Her father paused just long enough that Mirabelle glanced up at him. There was something in his face. In his tone. He knew more than he'd let on.

"Of course," her mother said, clucking her tongue. "My dear, you are a pastor's daughter. You are well respected in this community, and your reputation is worth more than all the gold in a king's treasury."

"I highly doubt that," Mirabelle said, unable to hide the hint of sarcasm. "But I do understand that you both love me and want what you think is best for me."

"We do," her father agreed. He smiled at her then, broadly, and turned to include her mother in the look. "I have some exciting news," he said. "It might even make you feel better."

"What's that?" her mother asked.

Mirabelle didn't like the fact that her father was changing the subject. In truth, it just upset her more. But she resumed her dishwashing while listening.

"I got a letter in the mail," her father said. "From another pastor out in Oregon I knew years ago. His son is traveling around, place to place, while learning if a life of missionary work is the one for him before he finds his own place to settle."

He stepped closer to Mirabelle. The sudden motion sent a chill through her. She sensed she was not going to like what he said next. Nervously, she bit her lip. "Oh?"

"Yes. His son is coming here. As I recall, the man was a good one. I'm sure his son will be just the same. Now, Mirabelle, I know you worry about your future. I do. But this might just be an opportunity for you. This young man, his name is Tom Hudson. He may just be your future husband. You will spend time with him and see if that is the case, as I hope it will be."

The teacup slipped from Mirabelle's fingers, but luckily landed in the water. No one noticed. Her head felt light, her stomach sick. Surely, surely, her father wouldn't try to marry her off to a man none of them knew! Why, that would be far worse than being married to a gunslinger.

She fought to control her trembling fingers. Luckily, the sudsy water gave her cover, and her mother's gasp and sudden clap of hands drew her father's attention.

"When will he arrive? We've so much to do," she said, her head swiveling around as she glanced about the room. "Where will he stay?"

"He'll have to stay in town at the hotel," her father said. "But I'm sure he'll be here for meals, for services. Just for socializing."

Her mother fixed her with a look that made Mirabelle's eyes widen. "And perhaps more. You'll just put all thoughts of that gunslinger out of your mind and focus on the pastor's son," she said firmly. "Your parents know best."

They left the kitchen before Mirabelle could come out of her stupor to respond. Angrily, she finished the dishes, wiped her hands dry, and took herself on a walk. Were all parents so sure that their way was the one and only and best path for their children? Or was it simply because her father was a pastor and had high standards?

What she'd said earlier she knew was true. Without a doubt, they loved her, and she understood that. But when it came to love...a love like her parents had, couldn't she choose for herself where she felt her heart leading her? When she thought about the future, it wasn't this Tom Hudson who came to mind, but Billy.

It was Billy's life she'd like to see about sharing. Or, at least to have the opportunity to discover if it was something she'd like.

Sighing, Mirabelle walked along the sidewalk, letting herself gaze into the store windows. She paused when the smell of freshly baked bread hit her nose. She had her purse with her. Perhaps she'd stop at the bakery and get herself something as a treat, or something as a peace offering for her parents.

The idea agreed with her, and she crossed the street and went into the bakery. A man was in front of her with a small child on each side of him. She patiently waited for her turn, paying them no mind while her eyes browsed the selection of cookies, rolls, and other baked goods.

"Anything else?" the baker asked as he filled a large bag.

Mirabelle tried not to stare. She'd never seen someone buy so much before. She couldn't tell who it was. The man had his hat on, and she didn't recognize the children.

"That's it," the man answered. He handed the bag to the boy and then chucked the little girl under the chin as he bent low. "Now, you all take that to your pa. I hope he recovers from his accident. If your family starts getting hungry again, you come find me right away. I'll make sure you have all you need."

The little girl threw her arms about the man's neck, and it knocked off his hat. Without thinking, Mirabelle stooped to pick it up, and found herself frozen, looking right into the eyes of Billy.

Neither of them moved until the baker asked, "Help you, Miss Blackstone?"

"Ah, yes," Mirabelle stammered, and released the hat. Billy's fingers brushed against hers, and she tried not to shiver at the warm tingles now racing over her skin. "Three apple tarts, please. I'll take them home."

"Of course." The baker turned and reached into the case.

"That was kind of you to do," Mirabelle said softly to Billy, as she nodded toward the retreating children.

"They're good people," he answered. "I'd do more for them if I could. Their pa is proud, though. Even if he's injured right now and out of work. But bread for work? That he agrees to. Once he's well, he'll also be one of my ranch hands. Lost his wife a few years back, needs a good steady job."

"Here you are," the baker interrupted.

Mirabelle paid him, and she and Billy moved to the door naturally, walking as one. The two children had run out already.

"What sort of work could those two do?" she asked. "The boy is what...six? His sister younger."

Billy nodded. "That's right." He grinned at her. "I'd tell you, but I don't want folks thinking I'm too soft."

When he laughed, Mirabelle did too. There was something about the sound that made her heart feel lighter. "Tell me," she pleaded.

He pushed up his hat. "Well, I had them mind my horse while I went to the store."

"Oh?" She raised a brow at him. "I sense there's more."

His smile grew wider. "Asked them to taste some candies for me, give me their opinions. I wasn't sure which I'd like best, of the penny candies. So, bought a sack and asked them to report back to me later so I'd know next time which colors were the best."

Mirabelle's heart just about melted. "No wonder that little girl hugged you," she said. "That was a very sweet thing to do, Mr. Madison."

"Billy, please," he told her, his eyes capturing her. "I'd like to be on a first-name basis with you."

Mirabelle's heart did a little flutter. She'd already been thinking of him as Billy. Perhaps things had just the smallest chance of working out.

"You must call me Mirabelle," she said shyly, her cheeks warming.

The way that he whispered her name as he bid her goodbye, caressing each letter while his eyes captivated her, echoed in her head for the rest of the day.

Chapter 7

"He really said that?" Gavin tipped his chair back as he kicked his legs on top of the porch rail.

"Sure did," Billy agreed. He didn't bother to mask his sigh. "I think she likes me, though."

"Every woman likes you," Gavin said, giving Billy a critical look. "I think it's that blond hair of yours. That angelic baby face."

"I don't have a baby face," Billy grumbled as he ran his hand over his jaw. Gavin might be right—he'd never been able to grow a beard, but that didn't matter right now. What mattered was the problem of Mirabelle Blackstone. Well—she wasn't the problem. Her father was.

"I bet he doesn't even let me get close to her," Billy said.

"She that important that you want to chase her?" Gavin asked, his brows raised.

Billy was quiet for a long moment. He wasn't sure how to explain it to Gavin. It wasn't that he thought his friend would tease him or laugh, it just was hard to put his feelings and the strange mixture of thoughts into some sort of semblance of order. When he saw Gavin still staring at him, he tried.

"It doesn't make sense, I know it," Billy said. "But just like how I knew I needed to leave home, how I knew I needed to go to that saloon the night we met, the way I knew that Barton the Bush was going to rob the post office, I just know. The first time I saw her, I knew. Of course," he added, "that doesn't mean a heap of beans if her pa says no."

Gavin threw his legs down and picked up his fiddle. Billy let himself lean back and listen to his friend play. It was low, mournful. It matched his emotions perfectly. Somehow, Gavin always did that. He'd about made up his mind to take a short doze when a distant puff of dust caught his attention.

"Visitor," Billy said, straightening up. He checked his belt, though his weapon never left his side. Even when he'd been helping to protect Hannah and her kids, he'd had it with him. No one under his protection would be without the best he could give—that included his friend, and he knew Gavin felt and behaved the same.

"Don't recognize the horse." Gavin frowned. "Old hat."

"Wait! I think that's Eli," Billy said and jumped up. "Must be one of his new mares."

Sure enough, his friend was riding closer. "What are you doing here?" Gavin asked as Eli came to a stop and jumped off the bay.

"An errand. Two, actually." Eli grinned. "Come to think of it, three."

He reached into a saddlebag. "Meg's made cookies. She insisted I deliver them to her uncles."

Billy looked at the wrapped bundle and then took it, opening it. Meg wasn't really their niece, but being on account Eli had been their best friend for a long time, when he married and claimed Meg and her little brother, Benjamin, as his own, they were added to the family, and he and Gavin had become uncles.

"They edible?" Gavin asked, looking at the black lumps with a little suspicion.

"They are if you know what's good for you," Billy grunted. Then he took one of the very overbaked cookies. "I forgot. You don't have a little sister. You got to eat what they make, hope it doesn't poison you, and tell them they did good. They expect it."

"Especially when they are only five," Eli said, nodding at the charred treats. "I ate three. You'll survive one."

Billy dunked his in his mug of cider, while Gavin picked one up and gingerly bit it, wincing. "We don't have a dentist in town," he grumbled.

"Hush. Tell her I've never tasted anything like it," Billy proclaimed.

"I was going to say that." Gavin frowned.

"So, you think of something else." Billy shrugged.

His friend got a slow smile on his face. "You tell her, Uncle Gavin says to bring him and Billy as many as she wants. Billy can't get enough of them, and I'm willing to give him my share."

Billy groaned and flopped down in his rocking chair. "All right, all right." He looked at Eli. "What else did you come for?"

Eli leaned against the rail. "Second, Hannah wants you for dinner soon."

"Anytime," Gavin said. Billy nodded.

There was quiet, and Billy squinted. "What aren't you saying?" he asked. He crossed his arms. "I hate when you do that."

Eli rubbed a hand on his jaw. The elected leader of their trio, his words and mannerisms carried a lot of weight. Billy could sense the next words weren't directed toward him and relaxed slightly. Gavin, meanwhile, had tensed.

"Spit it out," Gavin growled.

Eli shrugged. "The town wants a new sheriff."

"What's that have to do with us?" Billy asked.

"A few people have suggested Gavin," Eli answered.

Billy nodded slowly. "I can see that. You'd be perfect, really," he said to his friend.

"I'm not looking to be a sheriff," Gavin said. "That's a little too respectable. Once you go there, you don't return. I like who I am, and that's not going to change."

"I didn't know you were unrespectable," Eli said.

"The ladies don't know that," Gavin said with a wink.

Billy guffawed. Of them all, Gavin was least likely to ever settle. So, what was he worried about his reputation for?

"There's a meeting tomorrow afternoon in town at the church. Make sure you're there. It's at four." Eli pushed off the porch. "I'd better head on back. See you then."

"Give Hannah and the kids our love," Billy said.

He watched as Eli rode away, then returned to his chair. "Meeting at the church," he muttered. "Might get to see Mirabelle."

He caught Gavin's look and shrugged. "What? Just saying."

***

If the entire town had turned out for the meeting, Billy wouldn't have been surprised. Children were running around outside, women stood in clusters, and the men did as well. Everyone was talking. It sounded like a hive of bees all buzzing around.

He and Gavin rode up and tied their horses to a post. Slowly, they walked around until they spotted Hannah and Eli. As Billy hugged Hannah, he asked, "Kids here?"

"No, they stayed home with Gus," Hannah said. "Meg wanted to bake you more cookies." She looked at Gavin. "Did Eli tell you the town wants to nominate you?"

Gavin nodded, but didn't say anything. Not even a crack about Meg's cookies. Billy knew his friend was feeling tense and decided not to say anything. Besides, there was something else on his mind right now.

Billy let his eyes roam over the crowd. He was hoping to find Mirabelle. He knew she'd be here. After all, she lived in the house next to the church. Surely, she'd be here with her mother in some capacity, helping with something or other. That's what he always saw her doing.

Women, Billy reflected, were the real backbone of the community. They were always there in their quiet ways, doing this or that. Those things men wouldn't think about doing but made such a difference. Like setting out drinks or some food. Making sure there were blankets or bandages in times of need.

It always amazed him how every single woman he'd ever known—his ma and sisters included—seemed to have a sense of doing things before they needed doing. It spoiled a man, he thought. When you were sick, they knew just when you needed a drink, your favorite food. The memories washed over him, and a lump filled his throat.

He really ought to send his ma a letter. See how she was. Though he hadn't been living under her roof for a long time, it didn't mean he didn't love her any less. More—if anything.

Billy's gaze continued to roam across the lawn. What would his family think, him considering settling down? A smile started to form, but just as quick he gritted his teeth when Pastor Blackstone walked past, his wife at his side.

They paused to speak to someone just as the mayor, a tall, leggy fellow with a mustache that curled on each end, called, "Meeting time!"

Billy followed the others into the church and sat next to Gavin, though his eyes still sought Mirabelle. When she walked into the chapel and sat next to her mother, his heart sped up.

She looked beautiful. She was wearing a soft pink dress that complimented her perfectly. He hardly had time to admire her before she twisted her head, as if she knew he was looking at her, and stared right at him.

Billy couldn't stop the silly grin on his face. Her cheeks pinked, and she looked away shyly.

What did that mean?

He hardly paid attention to the town meeting. Only enough to follow along that the town wanted to elect a new sheriff. No one had come forward to volunteer, so names were being suggested to take the role. One everyone agreed on was Gavin. There hadn't even been another name mentioned.

His friend had stood, thanked the crowd for their confidence in him, and promised to think about it.

Billy understood his hesitation. Gavin wasn't wanting to take on a position where he'd be tied down. Sure, he'd bought land, but land didn't hold a man in one place. It could always be sold or entrusted to another, but a job? One thing Gavin—any of them—always did was finish what they started. That meant Gavin wouldn't leave the post until he was unable to work.

It was a lot to think about, and Billy would have felt the same if it were him. The folks were right, though. They needed a sheriff.

When the meeting ended, Billy hurriedly pushed himself toward where he'd seen Mirabelle leaving the church. When he stepped outside, he looked quickly in multiple directions.

There, he was rewarded when the voice of an angel asked, "Looking for me?"

Chapter 8

Billy jerked his head toward her, and smiled at Mirabelle. "I was," he agreed.

She stood there shyly, both hoping he'd say something and that no one would interrupt them. He cleared his throat. "How, ah, are you?"

"I'm good," she answered. Then, before she could stop herself, she said, "No, not really. But, I'm glad to see you."

His eyes were locked on hers. "I'm glad you are. I know we don't know each other, but I wanted to change that. There's this feeling I have that you and I could be something special."

Her chest tightened, and Mirabelle struggled to breathe. She wasn't used to anyone being so direct. Somehow, it didn't unsettle her.

Billy continued, "I asked your father if I could call and he said no." His eyes were searching hers. To see how she'd reply?

Mirabelle nodded. "Yes. I know. He...he picked out someone for me, but I don't like him."

"That doesn't seem right," Billy said. He crossed his arms. "Shouldn't you get a say in that? Choose who you want?"

"I think I should," Mirabelle said. She pressed her lips together.

"What's he like?" Billy asked. Then he grinned. "Curious about the competition, I guess. Hoping I still have a chance to best him out."

"I've only seen him briefly, at dinner last night," Mirabelle said. She closed her eyes to prevent a sigh, then opened them. "I know it sounds silly, but there's something about him I don't trust."

Billy's eyes sharpened. "Any reason why?"

She shook her head. "Just a feeling. I know it doesn't make sense. But maybe it's like how you just know you want to know me better. How...I feel that too." She stopped, feeling flustered. She was sure Billy would laugh, make fun of her. Anxious. She was feeling anxious. That must be why she'd admitted that she wanted to get to know him, too.

To her surprise, he was frowning. Billy reached out, brushed his fingers against hers, and pulled back. "Makes perfect sense. It's called intuition. My gut has saved me on more than one occasion. If you need help, if something isn't right, come get me. I mean it. I'll help you, no matter what."

"I will," Mirabelle whispered. She wanted to tell him thank you, to tell him that her father's actions weren't hers. That she wanted, more than wanted, to spend time with him, but the words froze in her mouth.

Callie walked up just then. "There you are," she said. Her eyes glanced between Mirabelle and Billy. "Your parents are looking for you," she said in a low voice.

"Better go," Billy said quietly. He tipped his hat and stepped back a few steps. "Remember. If you need help, let me know."

He walked away, but Mirabelle couldn't stop herself from watching him go.

"What was that about?" Callie asked, her eyes wide.

"I just...I told him that I wasn't too sure about the man Papa is interested in me getting to know." Mirabelle twisted her dress around her fingers. "I get a bad feeling from him."

"Didn't he just come to town?" Callie asked. "Maybe you just need to know him better. He's sure handsome-looking."

"Maybe on the outside," Mirabelle said. "But I'm not so sure on the inside. While I can't say I've met too many pastors' sons, he doesn't seem much like one."

Callie took her arm, and they walked across the church lawn. "What do you mean?" Her eyes were serious.

"He makes fun of people. Like Mrs. Stover, the general store owner. He made fun of the way she walked. He's rough in his talk and just...he just doesn't seem Christian-like. Like how you'd think a pastor's son would be."

"That's no reason to discount him," Callie said. "Maybe he's feeling awkward. Could be he didn't even want to come."

"Maybe," Mirabelle said quietly.

But maybe not.

"There you are," Mirabelle's father said, walking up with Tom Hudson, the man he wanted her to spend time with, alongside him.

"Yes. I was just talking with Callie," Mirabelle said.

"Why don't you and I go for a walk?" Tom asked her. "You can show me around a little more."

"That's a wonderful idea," her father agreed.

Mirabelle didn't think so herself, but put on a smile and nodded. Tom offered his arm and she took it, and they slowly started down the street.

"Is there anything in particular you'd like to see in the town?" she asked.

"Just the usual things," Tom said, his eyes reading each sign as they passed. As they neared the post office, he slowed. "Many people work inside of here?"

"Oh, just the postman and his wife," Mirabelle said, wondering at the odd question. "We aren't so large a town as there's ever too much mail."

They continued on past the diner, the barber, near the bank, and the hotel. "I hope your room is nice at the hotel," Mirabelle said, trying to ease the strained silence.

"Good enough," Tom answered. "I can see the bank from there. It's a good location."

She thought that was a strange thing to comment on, but didn't say anything.

"Many people work there?" he asked.

"At the hotel?" she answered, confused.

"No, the bank."

"I, ah, I don't know," Mirabelle said. "I've never been inside."

"Maybe you should go," he encouraged.

She didn't answer. What did one say to something so unusual?

"I didn't see anyone there at the sheriff's office," he said as they passed. "Looked empty. Guess you don't have a lot of trouble here?"

"Oh! Yes, well, we don't have a sheriff right now," Mirabelle said. "That's why we had the town meeting today."

His comment puzzled her. After all, hadn't he been at the meeting? He hadn't sat with her family, but she was sure he'd been nearby.

"That's right, that's right."

He didn't look like he was really listening to her. Mirabelle frowned. Was this what it would be like with a man like him around? Him always asking questions but never listening to the answers? It was a stark contrast to Billy, who listened, giving her all of his attention like nothing else mattered.

"What's over there?" Tom asked, pointing behind the stage office.

"There's not much. If you follow it down a short distance there's a stream, but it's dried up right now. We have had a really dry year," Mirabelle said.

"Let's go look at it," Tom suggested.

They walked to the stream, and Mirabelle shot a glance or two at him. Tom had dark hair, bright green eyes, and a rounded chin with a neat beard. Callie thought he was handsome, but she didn't think so. She much preferred Billy, with his blond hair and polite way of treating her.

They looked at the dry creek bed. "Goes on for a ways," Tom mused, rubbing at his chin. "Leads to the next town, I bet. Stones in the bed, no dirt or grass."

"I suppose? I don't know, really," Mirabelle said. "I've never followed it."

He turned to her then. "You're pretty," he said, and grinned. "Your pa seems to think we'd make a fine match." He grabbed at her arm and tugged her closer. "I agree."

"My pa," Mirabelle said, wrestling to free herself, "doesn't get to decide everything I do."

A flash of anger came into his eyes. "Oh? Well then, you'll do what *I* tell you to."

"I will not!" Mirabelle gasped and tried to step back. "How dare you say such a thing! We hardly know each other."

"You will, if you know what's good for you, and your family," he told her, squeezing her elbow.

His voice was calm, an incredible contrast to the grip he had on her, and Mirabelle winced at the pain. Her arm hurt so much, it took a moment for her to realize what he'd just said.

Her...family?

Instinct kicked in, and Mirabelle cried out and lashed at him, kicking him in the shin. When he swore loudly and released his hold on her, she ran back toward the town, to the safety of her home.

She had been right. Something was wrong with that man. Even worse was her family, and the entire town, might be in danger from him. Mirabelle didn't know how, but her instinct told her it was so. Her arm ached, and she held it tightly to her as she ran faster than she'd ever done in her life. She had to get home. Had to warn them.

Tears were rolling down her cheeks as she burst into the house.

"Goodness," her mother gasped at the sight of her. "What ever is wrong?"

"That man is horrible," Mirabelle cried out. "He hurt me!" she showed the bruising on her arm.

"Who hurt you?" her mother asked.

Footsteps drew closer, and her father walked into the small family room. "What's all the noise? What's happened?"

"Tom Hudson," Mirabelle said, turning her pleading expression to her parents. "He hurt me."

"I would never do that," Tom answered.

Mirabelle turned in shock. He was standing in the doorway, a look of sorrow on his face. Had she not seen him just moments before with venom in both his voice and eyes, she'd have believed his expression genuine.

"Why, if you've a bruise on your arm, I'm sorry. But when you tripped and I reached to grab you, your safety was my first thought. I suppose I used a little more strength than necessary," Tom said apologetically. "I'd never knowingly hurt you."

Mirabelle gaped at him. Her mouth opened and closed. "B-but—"

Her father fixed her sternly with his gaze. "I know you are unhappy about this situation. That it's not one of your choosing, but you have embarrassed yourself, your mother, and me with these false allegations."

"But, Papa!"

"No. It is a sin to lie, Mirabelle. You, of all people, should know this. You owe Tom an apology. One that you've thought a while on. You will go to your room right now, and you will stay there until you apologize."

"Apologize?" Mirabelle drew herself up. "I have nothing to apologize for! I'm not lying."

"And I'm not arguing," her father said, shaking his head.

He pointed upward and, pushing her way past both her father and Tom, Mirabelle ran out of the room with angry tears in her eyes.

As she hurried to her bedroom and shut the door behind her, leaning against it and trembling, she felt lost. Betrayed. What was happening? Why wouldn't her parents believe her? And worse...what was she going to do?

Chapter 9

Whistling to himself, Billy mounted his horse and headed the short distance to town. He was hoping there were some replies to his ad for additional ranch hands for him and Gavin. Right now, they had four, but since Billy had decided to pursue ranching, like Eli had, he figured eventually a dozen men would be needed.

As he rode to town, he let his mind wander along with his gaze. It was nice out. Giant white clouds that were soft and fluffy covered the bright blue sky. A gentle breeze blew across his face, carrying the scent of the earth and sunshine. Everything felt right. Except for the fact he didn't have Mirabelle as his own.

Billy stifled his sigh. It wasn't manly to moon over her, but he couldn't help it. It was also upsetting, both the fact she seemed to want to get to know him as well, and the fact her pa had decided someone else would be a better fit.

A frown creased Billy's face. He hadn't liked the look Mirabelle wore when she'd dropped her voice and told him she didn't care for the man her father wanted her to be with. He hoped she'd listen to her instincts. If something was wrong, he also hoped she'd tell him so he could do something about it.

The town rose before him, and Billy hurried. The sooner he did his errands, the sooner he could waste a little time in town, in hopes he'd run into Mirabelle.

He hurried into the post office. "Morning, Carl," he said. "Any letters?"

"Several," the postmaster said, handing over a thick stack.

Billy accepted them and wandered outside before he dropped himself on the bench right outside the door. He thumbed through the letters until his eyes widened at a familiar handwriting. "I'll be," he said, opening the letter quickly.

A pang of homesickness and happiness filled him as he read.

Dearest brother,

I have a surprise for you! Guess who is coming to your town for a visit? Me! Isn't that exciting? I think it is.

I'll be there shortly after you get this letter. I miss you and can't wait to see you. I have been traveling, and your town is on my way home.

See you soon,

Nora

Nora. She was coming? Billy sat up and smiled. Nora was his older sister, but only by a year. The two of them had been inseparable growing up. A clever girl who grew into a capable woman, she had been entrusted to oversee many of their father's affairs when it came to business. Perhaps that was why she was passing through.

He stood, but then hesitated. Did he need to do something special for her arrival? There was an extra room at the house for her if she wanted it. Unless she'd prefer the hotel. She might, seeing as she didn't know Gavin. What else did women need? He really wasn't sure, but wanted to have it on hand for her. Deciding it might be prudent to ask someone who would know, he crossed the street to the general store.

Mrs. Stover greeted him just as soon as the door opened. "Hello, Mr. Madison."

"Hello," Billy answered. "Say, my sister is coming to visit for a few days. Any idea if there's something I should have on hand for her? Being a bachelor, I figured I'd better ask before she shows up and scolds me."

The shopkeeper laughed. "You are a thoughtful brother," she said approvingly. Then she added, "I'd suggest, if you don't already have it, get some tea, cookies, and have a bit of food on hand. Things either of you can make simply, for a nice meal. Some good soap, and have you bedding for her?"

Billy nodded. "Bedding, yes. But give me the rest. Whatever you think is best."

"I certainly will," Mrs. Stover promised, and busied herself for a few moments filling several bags. "This should do it," she said.

"Thank you," Billy said gratefully, and paid. He carried it out to his horse and started stuffing everything into his saddlebags.

A young woman was passing, and he stopped to see if it was Mirabelle. It wasn't. Disappointed, he looked away, then back at her. It was the girl he'd seen with Mirabelle the day the town had been talking about their need for a sheriff.

"Hello," he greeted. "Aren't you Mirabelle's friend?"

She paused and smiled. "Hello. Yes."

"You wouldn't happen to know if Mirabelle is nearby, would you?" Billy asked.

The woman shook her head. "No, she's not. Mirabelle..." She bit her lip, seemingly nervous.

A lump of worry formed in Billy's gut. "What?" he asked, tensing.

"I'm Callie, her best friend," she said, by way of reintroduction. "Mirabelle is being kept in her room. She's only allowed to go to church."

"Why?"

Callie lowered her voice. "She made an accusation against someone. The man they want her to marry. That's all she was able to tell me. She said he hurt her. I believe her, but her parents don't."

Fury filled Billy. Mirabelle, hurt? "How was she hurt?" he asked, his voice thick. Instinct was telling him to rush to her, but his years as a gunslinger were forcing him to wait, to gather information and remain calm.

"I don't know," Callie whispered. "But she was very shaken when she told me. Her mother came and dragged her away. I've not seen her since Sunday."

It was Friday now. Billy frowned.

That meant Callie hadn't seen her for a while.

"If you can, pass along a message. Tell her I'm going to see how I can help."

"I will," Callie promised. "I'd better go. But I'll tell her."

Billy nodded. He felt tense. That same sort of anticipation filled him like it always did before something big. He drummed his fingers on his thigh, then mounted his horse. There were a lot of thoughts spinning around in his mind right now, but just like a tornado, he had no idea which way they were going to land.

He shifted slightly on his mare, then squinted. Someone was coming out of the bank.

"Callie," Billy called.

She wasn't far away and turned. Billy rode to her. "That him?" he asked softly, jerking his head toward the man who looked familiar.

"Yes. That's the man her parents want her to marry," Callie whispered, then she vanished into a store.

Billy urged his horse into a slow walk. The man wasn't paying much attention to his surroundings, instead too focused on the outside of the bank. He was walking around it, looking at each side. Something wasn't setting right inside of Billy. Not with the man nor his actions.

Taking a deep breath, Billy filed it away for later. He'd talk to Gavin about this and get his opinion. He wheeled his horse around and rode slowly past the church and the house Mirabelle lived in. Though he went slowly and took long looks, he didn't see her anywhere.

Feeling worried, he kicked his horse into a trot. Something was about to happen. The air was filled with the kind of tension in it that was more than familiar to him. The problem right now was the question of who was going to get hurt.

He was not about to let that be Mirabelle.

Chapter 10

Watching from her window, Mirabelle thought she saw Billy pass by. Had he been looking for her? She couldn't tell, but he'd gone slowly, and his head had been craned and twisted as he looked around.

Mirabelle had waved frantically, but wasn't sure he'd seen her, not with the large oak outside blocking most of the view.

She hoped he had been looking for her. After almost a week of being a prisoner in her room, Mirabelle was bordering on desperate. Desperate to get outside, desperate to ask Billy for help, desperate to figure out what was going on.

Twice, she'd had dinner with her parents and Tom. She'd remained quiet for most of the meal. Tom, however, had not. He'd asked all sorts of questions that didn't make sense to her, and her parents had eagerly answered every one of them. That didn't sit right with her. In fact, it made Mirabelle wonder all the more if perhaps Tom wasn't quite who he'd said he was.

Why would a pastor's son ask so many questions about the town, she had asked her mother later. Her mother had clucked at her, and said that's what a pastor must do. Become familiar with the town and the people.

She supposed that was a valid point. But still...her intuition told her something wasn't right.

Of course, she couldn't do a thing about that or prove it one way or the other unless she got out of her room. And to do so, that meant that she had to apologize.

Mirabelle didn't know what to do. She hadn't lied. If she apologized, even though she wasn't sorry, was that lying? She wasn't sure. But the one thing she was sure of was sitting in her room was just giving Tom longer to act on whatever plan he had.

So, apologize she must.

Quietly, Mirabelle went down the stairs. Both her parents looked as she entered the small kitchen. Her mother wore a look of hope, her father one of sternness.

"I promise not to speak ill of the man you've chosen for me and to give him a chance."

The words left her lips and she felt better. It wasn't an apology at all. It was a fact, though they seemed to accept it as an apology. She also had not lied. She was going to give him a chance all right, to prove just what kind of a man he was.

Her father looked relieved, which she found a little odd. Her mother rushed over and hugged her. "That's my darling girl," she cooed. "I bet you feel much better now, don't you?"

"I do," Mirabelle agreed. It was the truth. It was nice being out of her room. Now, she simply had to get word over to Billy, somehow, and tell him what had happened. What she suspected.

"You look a little pale without sunshine," her mother said. "I know just what you need. You'll go to the ladies auxiliary basket luncheon next week."

"With Tom," her father added.

Mirabelle stiffened, then she nodded. "Of course, Papa. I will happily take a basket, and perhaps Tom will bid on it. After all, the money goes to those in need. Every man must bid. I'm sure he'd be willing to do that to have lunch with me. If he doesn't win, why, then it's just a short time apart." She put on her most winning smile, which seemed to set her mother at ease.

Secretly, Mirabelle hoped Billy would be there and win instead. How could she make that happen?

"May I go and visit Callie?" Mirabelle asked.

"No," her father answered. "Stay here. Help your mother with dinner."

It was still hours before dinner. Mirabelle looked at her father, then slowly nodded. When she glanced at her mother, there was a confused look upon her face as well.

Tom walked in then with a smile. "Yes, let's all visit a while," he said. "Tell me about this luncheon."

Mirabelle's mother started happily talking. To keep busy, Mirabelle went and got the ingredients out to start making a dessert to go with dinner. She was acutely aware of Tom's eyes on her the entire time, but each time she turned, he wasn't looking at her.

Unease filled Mirabelle. She hoped that Tom would just leave and go somewhere else. Find someone else.

A shiver came over her the next time she turned, to reach for the kettle to pour tea. Tom was looking at her father in a cold and calculating way. Trying to pretend as though she hadn't noticed, Mirabelle brought tea and coffee to the table, serving it.

She had the strangest sensation then that she wasn't the only one prisoner in the house. But how could that be?

The evening dragged on. Mirabelle and her mother made dinner, and her father and Tom stayed in the kitchen once it had been eaten and the women washed the dishes. Mirabelle wanted to ask what was going on, but her mother didn't seem as though anything was bothering her. Her father though, he seemed slightly stiffer. More concerned, as he leaned over the pages of a sermon he was creating, titled *Do Unto Others*.

Tom was looking at the paper every now and then, as if watching to see what he was writing. Did that mean that he was watching each move any of them made? She had to alert Billy, but wasn't sure how. Mirabelle hoped Callie would stop by so she could slip her a message.

Something was seriously wrong. She didn't know what, but all her hopes now rested on the gunslinger. As she closed her eyes that night and whispered her bedtime prayers, the only thing that seemed to come out was, *Please. Protect my family.*

Chapter 11

"Hurry up! I don't want to be late," Billy called from the wagon.

"I'm coming. Couldn't find my better hat." Gavin came out of the house and shut the door behind him. He mounted his horse and the two set out toward town.

"You sure think your sister is going to want to stay here or at the hotel?" Gavin asked.

"I don't know. But either way, I'm ready," Billy said. "That's why I have the wagon. It's been a few years. I wonder what she looks like."

"I'm sure you two will have a lot of catching up to do," Gavin remarked. "I'm going to go talk to the mayor a little once we get into town."

"Made up your mind yet about being sheriff?" Billy asked.

"Not yet. Have a few questions I want to ask, though," Gavin answered. "It's a serious thing. A big commitment."

Billy knew that. Which is why he wasn't pushing Gavin to answer one way or another. It was his choice, but it was also something that had the potential to change Gavin's life. Eli had urged him to take all the time he needed to think it over, and that's just what Gavin said he planned to do.

"What about you?" Gavin looked over at Billy.

"What about me?" Billy asked.

"You and Mirabelle. Thought any more about that?"

It was hard not to snort at the question. Of course he'd thought about her. The problem was, each time he'd ridden slow-like past the church or her house, he hadn't seen her. He hadn't seen Callie either, and he couldn't spend all day in town. Things needed tending to back home as well. He spent long enough there each day to be assured he heard the news, people knew he was around, and that any gossip fell in his ears.

So far, he'd heard nothing about Mirabelle.

Of course, that meant that he felt helpless, more often than not. It was a terrible thing being attracted to a woman, knowing she was interested in you, but not being able to act because of a third person. Especially when that person was one her father thought was more suitable. Billy longed for a chance to prove his love.

Perhaps he'd get it, Eli had told him, as they'd discussed what Callie had told Billy that day. He reminded him that sometimes, nothing brought two people together like a heap of trouble. Billy supposed that could be true. After all, for Hannah and Eli, it sure was.

Was it possible there would be a happy ending for him and Mirabelle?

Several times, he'd seen the other pastor's son. Each time he did, he grew more suspicious of the man. He seemed to spend a lot of time looking at the same few buildings, and then walking back to the dried-up creek bed. It had been hard to watch him and not be seen, not when everyone and their cousin wanted to stop and tell him hello, but Billy had managed. And hadn't liked the feeling that kept crawling up his spine.

Gavin was waiting patiently for his answer. Billy realized he'd been lost in thought. He nodded slowly.

"The first thing I want to do is talk with her," Billy said. "Right now, I don't even care about what I want, which is to get to know her better. My gut is telling me something is going on and she might be in danger. I want to make sure she's okay. I'm about to go to her house and just knock."

"You know I've got your back," Gavin said.

"I do. And I appreciate it," Billy said. "I saw there's a ladies auxiliary luncheon coming. I plan to go. Surely her mother will let her attend."

"Going to bid on her lunch?" Gavin asked.

"With all I've got, if I have to," Billy said grimly.

"Don't bet the ranch," Gavin said. "Remember, I own half."

They laughed, and Billy grinned. "There's another fifty acres coming up for sale. Was thinking we should get it."

"It's a good idea," Gavin agreed.

"There's the stage," Billy shouted, and hurried the horses along.

They separated a few moments later, Gavin leaving to meet with the mayor and Billy watching as passengers exited the stage.

"Billy!" A high, clear voice called, and a moment later, he was half knocked over from Nora's hug.

"Nora," he said, squeezing just as hard. He stepped back with a grin. "Aren't you a sight for sore eyes! I've missed you.

"I've missed you too," Nora said, hugging him again. "You look good, Billy. I was a little worried, honestly. You, being here alone."

"I'm not alone," Billy told her. "Like I write, Eli and Gavin are here, and Eli married."

Nora smiled. "I'm glad you have someone to keep you company." She pointed then to a small travel bag. "That's mine. Where's the hotel?"

"It's over here," Billy said, nodding his head. "But you are welcome to stay with me and Gavin."

"As much as I appreciate the offer," Nora said, "do you really want me to answer all Mama's questions about what your place is like and what you eat and how clean it is?"

Billy froze. And then he remembered why Nora was his favorite sister. "Hotel has a restaurant," he said, scooping up her bag. "Let's get you settled in and grab a bite."

Nora laughed, but didn't disagree. She put her arm through his, and they walked across to the hotel.

Just as they were about to go inside, he saw Mirabelle and frowned, missing a step. She was walking with the man he'd seen inspecting the bank, the man Callie had said was who her parents wanted her to be interested in. His rival.

Mirabelle didn't seem to notice him, but she looked miserable. A moment later, she disappeared.

Nora was looking at him, and he gave a weak smile. "Here we are! Let's get you checked in." Hopefully, she wouldn't ask who he'd been staring at.

He helped her get a room and waited patiently while she changed into a clean dress. Once Nora was ready, they went into the restaurant and sat down.

"It all looks good," Nora said. "Do you have a suggestion?"

"Chicken here is tasty," he offered.

"That's what I'll have then," she agreed.

Within moments, they were sitting before plates of fried chicken, mashed potatoes, green beans, and thick slabs of bread. Between bites, Nora filled Billy in on everything that had been happening back home.

When they each sat before a large slice of chocolate cake, Nora asked, "So, are you going to tell me who that woman was that made you look so worried?"

"What woman?" Billy asked.

"Just before we walked into the hotel. The girl with the other man."

Billy should have known that she'd noticed. Nora was observant. He took a bite and chewed slowly, trying to figure out how to answer her. Finally, he decided on the truth.

"She's the pastor's daughter."

"And?" His sister arched one perfect brow.

"And her father doesn't like me." Billy hated admitting that. He wasn't ashamed, but he didn't like how saying the words felt. They made him hurt. Angry.

"How does she feel about you?" Nora asked. "It's not the father you'd be courting."

The tips of Billy's ears turned red, he bet, judging by the heat he felt. He wished for his hat on to hide them. "I think she likes me too," he told her. "Just not had a chance to find out, not with that other man around."

"I didn't get a good feeling from the man she was with," Nora said. "Who is he?"

"That's something I'm not sure about," Billy said. He shook his head. "He claims to be the son of another pastor.

But there's something about him that doesn't set right. Mirabelle said she feels like something is wrong. I saw him acting strangely earlier. Poking around and looking like he was checking out the lay of the land."

"You would notice that," Nora said. "Are you sure that's what he's doing? That you aren't just imagining it? Seeing danger where there is none?"

"It's a good question." He frowned. "I don't think that's it, though. I have a feeling. I can't explain it, but that feeling isn't ever wrong. The thing I worry most about is Mirabelle. I've not had a chance to talk to her alone to make sure she's okay. A friend of hers said she'd been locked in her room for accusing him of hurting her."

Nora gasped. "Billy, you must do something," she said. "You can't let her be hurt."

"I plan to," he said. "In fact, formed a plan last night. There's a lunch auction by the ladies auxiliary coming up," he explained. "Highest bidder wins lunch with the one who made the lunch. I'll bid on her basket. When I win, I'll be able to make sure she's okay and see what she can tell me about what's going on."

"What makes you so sure you'll win?" his sister asked.

"I'll go as high as I have to," Billy said, fully aware ice had crept into his voice.

"Is that asking for trouble? From her father, I mean," Nora asked. "If he didn't want you to call on his daughter, will he allow you to have a meal with her?"

Billy considered for a moment, then shook his head. "Who would refuse a high bidder when the money goes to the needy? It's only lunch, and he can keep a close eye on us if he's worried about it. I'll still figure out a way to make sure she's okay."

"It's a good plan," Nora agreed. "How can I help?"

"Don't," Billy answered. "I can't let you get hurt. If this guy is bad news, I don't want him coming after you."

"That's no fun at all," his sister pouted. "Part of the reason I wanted to visit you was to have something interesting happen. It always does when you are around."

"You know," Billy said, as he pushed away his empty plate. "I'd be willing to trade all that."

"For what?" Nora asked, copying his movement.

"Mirabelle, and her safety."

Chapter 12

Mirabelle tried not to walk any slower than she was. However, she wasn't wanting to be out of sight of the town and witnesses, in case Tom hurt her again. Each time she remembered how he'd grabbed her arm, her stomach squeezed, and she felt nauseated.

She loathed being with him, but her parents—and Tom—had insisted that she join him on a stroll through town.

It seemed that their walks were always the same. Past the post office and near the bank and down to the dried-up creek. She was starting to form an opinion that he was looking for something, but didn't dare voice it to her parents. For one, she didn't think they'd listen. Next, Tom always seemed to be around. Even late into the night.

Mirabelle had realized last night that she and her mother hadn't been doing their typical activities, like helping tend to the community garden, visiting those sick or new with child, or calling on some of the churchgoers who didn't come to town often for one reason or another. Whenever her mother had suggested something or tried to leave, Tom was there with a reason why they should stay inside.

She really did think they were prisoners. It wasn't so much a fleeting thought now, but a concern. The way her parents exchanged glances now and again, Mirabelle wondered if it was possible they did notice something amiss. An additional question was, if they did, why hadn't they done anything about it?

They went past the post office, and Mirabelle stopped. There were new Wanted signs on the front. Just as she was taking a closer look, Tom reached past her and ripped one down.

"Why did you do that?" Mirabelle asked.

"Don't ask so many questions," he snapped, and hurried her along.

Tom led her toward the dry creek, and Mirabelle wished with all her heart Billy would come riding past. She longed to tell him her worries, ask him to investigate. As they stood there, Tom squinting in one direction, then the next, Mirabelle simply stood quietly.

He turned and faced her, studying her for a long moment. His nearness frightened her, and Mirabelle couldn't help the tremble that came over her. She didn't dare speak for fear of saying the wrong thing or making him angry. That seemed to please him, for he nodded at her approvingly.

"You know," Tom said, turning away and looking back at the creek. "I understand you've lived a sheltered life. One of service, and innocence." He faced her again. "But you are going to be my wife one day, and that means I tell you what to do and when. You'd better learn fast when to talk and when to shut up."

Mirabelle stiffened. She didn't like that one bit. Anger filled her. How dare he speak to her that way. And never had she made him think she planned to marry him. Where had he gotten that idea from? She longed to say something, to try and leave. But then practicality won out. There was no one around. She was alone with him. It was likely, even if she screamed for help, no one would hear her.

It would be far better to stay silent, to try to get back to town. There, she might see Callie or someone else who would sense something wrong. They might help her, and she could tell them how she feared she and her parents were being held hostage in some way.

Then, a thought came to mind. Perhaps if she played along, he'd be kinder. Let her go out alone at times. Even tell her why he kept coming here to the hotel, and the post office, the bank, and the creek. Tell her just why he thought they were going to marry. With that information, it was possible she'd have something she could pass along to be of use in stopping him from doing just whatever it was he intended.

It was worth trying.

Stepping closer, she smiled and gently rested a hand on his arm lightly before removing it. Carefully, in what she hoped wasn't a challenging tone but one of sweetness, Mirabelle asked. "Are we to marry? Papa hasn't told me that."

"I'm sure he will," Tom answered. He leaned over and scooped up a handful of pebbles. One by one, he threw them into the creek. "You'll come in handy."

Handy? That made her blink in surprise. That was certainly a strange way to refer to a potential bride. Did he mean her capabilities at keeping a house? Not that she'd do that for him. Mirabelle didn't plan to leave and go anywhere with him. Not willingly, anyway. She'd scream her head off or run away before that happened.

He was frowning into the distance, seemingly lost in thought. Mirabelle wasn't sure what to do. If she needed to find out more, to learn and understand why he made such cryptic statements, then she needed to pull it out from him. But how?

Almost at once, an image of Callie came to mind. From a young age, Callie had all of the men lavishing her with attention. One thing she'd always done was flatter them.

Perhaps Mirabelle could try that too. And without telling a lie.

Though, that might be hard. How could she flatter Tom?

The silence dragged on. Taking a deep inhale, Mirabelle forced a smile onto her face. "I like a man who knows what he wants. Your life seems so interesting. Where will we go after we marry? I'm tired of being in a small town with no excitement. You travel often, don't you? Will I go along as well?"

Tom turned to her, a pleased smile on his face at her interest. "I've sure seen a lot," he agreed. "Everything from mountains taller than you can imagine to unusual rock formations, underground caves that go so deep they swallow your lantern, and cities so busy you can stand on a corner for an hour and see a thousand people hustle past."

"My goodness," Mirabelle said. "Will we see those too?" She made her eyes as wide as she could when she asked.

"Maybe," Tom answered. He scratched at his jaw. "I'm leaving in a few days on business to Rustin. Once we're married, maybe we'll go there together. It's a big place. A lot of folks."

"I'd like that," Mirabelle said, giving him her sweetest smile.

He pulled her to him then, and roughly kissed her. Mirabelle wanted to pull away but didn't, even though the stale smell of him repulsed her. As quickly as he'd kissed her, he stopped and looked at her, his eyes narrowed.

Her heart nearly stopped, thinking he was glaring at her, when she realized he wasn't focused on her, but looking over her shoulder. A man stood a few yards away watching them. He looked vaguely familiar, even though Mirabelle was sure she'd never seen him before.

Tom strode forward. "What do you want?" he asked.

"Got a message for you," the man said, then spat in the dirt. He looked at Mirabelle. "When are you going to bring her to cook for us?"

"What?" she asked, confused by the question. Then, she recognized the man. "You're the person on the Wanted poster," she gasped. She took several steps backward.

"You're not going anywhere," Tom said. He grabbed her arm and pulled her into him. "You're going to keep your mouth shut, you hear?"

"Show her who's boss, boss," the other man snorted.

Boss? Mirabelle's eyes widened as she looked between the two. If the other man was a wanted criminal, then what did that make Tom?

"Shut it," Tom growled, looking at him. He turned back to Mirabelle. "This is your only warning. You keep what you saw to yourself, you got it?"

Mirabelle nodded frantically, her lips tightly closed. He squinted at her, and then before she could move, he struck her hard in the face.

"There's a lot more of that if you talk," he growled. "Time to go back. Hurry up."

Mirabelle didn't hesitate. Her feet led her away quickly, as she pressed one hand to her throbbing cheek. He hadn't struck her hard enough to split her skin, but there would be a bruise. Of that she was sure. At a half run, anxious to get away, her eyes scanned the street for someone to pass along a message to Billy.

Desperation filled her. There was no one, and soon, Tom would catch up to her. She had to find someone to help. Who knew when there'd be another chance? A sob caught in her throat and then wrenched free. How could the streets be empty right now? What was she to do?

Mirabelle wrapped her arms around herself. How could her father give her hand to such a cruel man, one who would hurt her and threaten her? She was sure Billy never would have done that. More sobs threatened to escape as she hurried. It would do no good to tell her parents. They wouldn't, couldn't, protect her. That was obvious.

She was on her own.

A woman came out of the general store just then, a package in her hand. Mirabelle didn't know her, but wished she did. Their eyes locked at the exact moment Tom grabbed her arm.

Panic filled Mirabelle. She'd wasted her chance. She was no longer able to seek help. Then, to her surprise, the other woman threw herself at her.

"There you are!" she wailed. "I'm desperate to talk to you! What am I going to do? How will I tell my mother? You must help me!" She dragged Mirabelle away from Tom, half turning and giving him an apologetic look. "I'm sorry. It's a female issue. I'm sure you understand?" She pulled Mirabelle toward the diner, loudly talking about how she was scared to visit the doctor, and what would her mother say.

Mirabelle wasn't sure what was happening and blinked rapidly. All she knew was Tom was as stunned as she was, and still stood there in the street while this strange woman hustled her into the diner with a surprisingly strong grip.

Chapter 13

Billy looked up from the Eli's kitchen table to smile at Meg, who had stuck her head around the corner. Hannah quickly pulled her away.

He, Gavin, and Eli were clustered around a pile of notices, with the remnants of coffee and cake before them.

Eli was marking points on a map. "Look at this. Seven robberies in the last two months. They are creeping closer, and Red Ridge is a possibility."

Nodding, Billy pointed out, "It's logical. We get a lot of money through here by stage and wagon."

Gavin sighed, "And I suspect everyone within miles knows we don't have a sheriff, either. It was in all the papers when the judge came through and settled things and got rid of the old one."

"That's why we need to be prepared to stop anything if there's an issue. We've built our homes here. No one is going to cause trouble for our people." Eli smacked his hand on the table. "I'm not letting anyone hurt my family. Hannah and the kids have been through too much. They deserve to have an easy life. One of peace."

There were no arguments there. Billy ran his hands through his hair. "We got any hints about what the gang looks like?" he asked. He didn't want to mention his suspicion of Tom Hudson without proof. It wouldn't be right, even though his gut was yelling at him something awful.

"Not yet," Eli said. "Still waiting."

"I'll do it," Gavin said, his voice low.

Billy looked at him. "Do what?"

"Acting sheriff, on a trial period." Gavin frowned. "Just as a trial. I wanted to settle down. Have a little peace for myself. Maybe more than that, eventually. I'm not sure which is the best thing for me—working as sheriff or saying no—or if I'd regret one over the other. I guess I won't know unless I try this."

Eli nodded. "Sometimes that's the only way. If Billy and I ride to some of the towns that were robbed to get more information, can you keep everyone safe here?"

"I will," Gavin promised. "The town, Hannah, and the kids."

"You've got me too," old Gus said, walking into the room. He sat heavily at the table. "You know I won't let nothing or nobody hurt 'em."

"I appreciate it, Gus," Eli said.

The old man grunted, and said, "How long you be gone?"

"No longer than we must," Eli said. He looked at Billy. "I know your sister is visiting. Will she mind?"

"Hopefully not. I'll explain what's going on. Knowing her, she'd tell me to go," Billy said.

Though his answer was one of nonchalance, in truth he was swallowing back his worry about leaving. He didn't want to be far from Mirabelle, just in case. Tom was a danger, and he wanted to protect her. Still, if a gang came shooting up the town, or if this gang belonged to Tom, he might be doing her a favor by stopping them.

The whole thing worried him. The air was filled with something dangerous. Billy shook his head. He didn't like this. Not one bit.

"Let's go now," Gavin said. "We might be back late tonight if we luck out and learn something quickly."

"Got any paper?" Billy asked Hannah, who came into the room. "I want to leave a note for my sister."

"I'll drop it at the hotel," Gavin offered. "I'm going to go talk to the mayor."

Billy scribbled a quick message to Nora. Hopefully, she wouldn't be mad at him she'd come all this way and he'd left.

Hannah bustled around the kitchen and had a bundle of food for them within moments. She hugged Eli tightly. "Please, be careful."

"I will," Eli promised, and kissed her.

Billy couldn't help feeling envious. He wished he was kissing Mirabelle right now. Would she be worried if she knew he was leaving town, and why? Then, he straightened. Who knows? Depending on what they found out, maybe she would be kissing him, and soon. And just maybe her father wouldn't do anything to stop it because he'd have gotten the bad guys cleared out of town and protected her.

What would life with Mirabelle by his side be like, he wondered? He didn't know, but he'd been admiring her for so long, Billy knew that he'd be the proudest man in the world with her on his arm. He wanted nothing more than to prove to her each day that she was special. That he loved her deeply.

Billy wished he could tell her that this very moment. What would she say if he did?

A moment later, he and Eli were speeding away to the next town. Dust rose behind them in large clouds.

"What do you think we'll find out?" Billy asked. He was trying not to feel impatient to hurry there and back, to check that Mirabelle was safe.

"Don't know," Eli answered. "I'm sure hoping something. If there's a gang about to come to our area, the more we know the better." He looked over at Billy. "You're thinking something."

"It's not a fact yet," Billy said. "Just a feeling."

"Feelings can be facts," Eli said. "What do you know?"

"Mirabelle Blackstone."

"Go on." Eli was giving him his full attention.

"She's concerned. Her parents have been forcing her to spend time with a man. She doesn't trust him, and neither do I. I've seen him walking around the outside of the bank, looking behind it, walking toward the creek and looking."

"The creek." Eli frowned. "One direction leads to Wayside. The other to Martinburg."

"It's dry out," Billy added. "No tracks walking on stones."

"She learn anything?" Eli asked.

"That's the problem. She went to her parents. Told them he'd hurt her, and they locked her in her room. I'm worried about her. I've been trying to see her but haven't been able to yet."

"I'll ask Hannah to check in on her," Eli said. "They wouldn't refuse a woman visiting her."

"Her best friend said she hadn't been allowed to see her. Not sure Hannah could get through," Billy said. "Especially because everyone knows she's your wife and you and I are friends."

Eli was quiet a moment. Finally, his voice broke through the horses' pounding hooves. "Mirabelle seems like a clever girl. I bet she's working on something."

***

Billy rubbed at his face. He was tired. So far, they'd talked to a dozen people and learned nothing. The sheriff was out somewhere, and hopefully he'd be along soon. It was getting dark, and Billy really wanted to get back. With some information, if possible.

"Sorry to keep you waiting," a man said, walking in. "Sheriff Buckwood. You men were asking about the gang going around hitting the banks and post offices?"

"That's right," Eli said, standing and offering his hand first. "We're concerned they are heading our way. Any information you can give might help us prevent it."

Billy offered his hand as well, then they all sat. "We only have an acting sheriff right now," he said. "Which is another reason we worry we might be a target."

"That's a good reason," Sheriff Buckwood said. "Less law, more crime."

"So far, our town has been protected," Billy said mildly, not wanting to let on just how they took care of their own. It was a fact that not everyone trusted gunslingers because not all of them were on the right side of the law.

"I can't tell you much," the sheriff said with a headshake. "I can tell you it's four men. Only got a good look at one of them."

"Anything you can tell us is better than nothing," Eli said.

"The one I saw was the front man. Seemed to be the brains. He was giving the orders. I'm not ashamed to admit I was caught unawares. He'd come in, talking to me, asking questions."

"What kind of questions?" Billy asked.

"Oh, said he was new to town. Asking where the hotel was, best place for a bite. All that. Said he was a traveling pastor."

Billy's head shot up. "That so?"

"I turned my back for a moment, next thing I woke up in my jail cell and the bank had been robbed." Sheriff Buckwood shook his head. "Bank manager told me there were four of them, and based on the description, the one who claimed to be the pastor was the one who carried away the cash."

"Slick," Eli said.

"Sure was," the sheriff said. "Wouldn't have ever suspected him."

"What did he look like?" Billy asked.

"About my height. He was actually real easy on the eyes. I bet the women love him. Dark hair, bright green eyes you wouldn't forget if you saw, and a well-groomed beard."

Billy felt a sickening jolt as he realized he'd seen a man just like that. He looked over at Eli. His friend tensed. "You've seen him."

"I sure have."

"When?" Eli stood, already moving for the door.

Close on his heels, Billy answered, "On Mirabelle's arm, claiming to be the son of a pastor."

Chapter 14

Mirabelle clutched the cup of tea in her hands. She could sense Tom staring—no, glaring at her—through the glass window, but hoped she was wrong. Still, she asked, "Is he watching me?"

"Yes," the other woman said. There was a concerned look on her face. "But he doesn't have a good view of us. He's outside and can't hear us, either."

"Thank you," Mirabelle whispered. She swallowed hard and noticed her hands trembling. Slowly, she set down the tea. "I...I need help."

"You can trust me," the woman said. Her eyes were clear, truthful. "My name is Nora Madison. I'm just visiting, but tell me what's going on, and I'll get help for you. You are hurt. I can see that. Your face—"

"Madison? Are you related to Billy?" Mirabelle asked, hope flaring in her for the first time that day. It was enough to make her forget the throbbing of her cheek.

"Yes, he's my little brother." Nora smiled. "Do you know him?"

"Not as well as I'd like," Mirabelle admitted, then was aware she was blushing.

"Ohhhh! I wonder," Nora said. She got a thoughtful look on her face, which grew into a teasing look. "Billy told me there was a woman he liked. I bet it's you."

Mirabelle didn't answer, but she knew her cheeks were bright red.

Nora laughed, leaned forward, and said, "I approve. I knew right away I'd like you. He also has a plan."

"What kind of a plan?" Mirabelle asked.

"He heard there is a picnic basket lunch. He's planning to bid on a basket," Nora said. Her eyes were filled with laughter. "He likes fried chicken."

"That's what I'll make," Mirabelle said with a smile. She bit her lip then in worry. "I hope he wins. I need to talk with him, desperately."

The humor left the other woman's eyes. "I can tell something is wrong. Can you tell me what? I know it's to do with that man who was with you. If I can't help, I can at least tell Billy what you've told me, and maybe he can do something. We won't leave you helpless."

"He did offer to help me," Mirabelle said. Her brow furrowed. "Do you think that he will?"

"Yes," Nora said. She nodded. "Billy's always rushed to be there for others. Big or small, it didn't matter what it was. If he felt like someone needed help, needed him, he was there. I think that's in part why he became a gunslinger. He felt a need to make a difference and said that sometimes a person was too restricted by being a lawman. There were rules to follow and he hated that, hated standing by and watching people be hurt when the law's hands were tied."

"I can understand that," Mirabelle said. "It infuriates me as well. Where is the justice, when those who should be protected suffer from delays?"

Nora gave a sad smile. "It's true. I hope one day that changes, but I'm not sure it will."

Mirabelle took a deep breath. She closed her eyes briefly, then opened them again. "I don't know how he can help. I only know something is going on, but I don't know what. It's odd, and doesn't quite sound...real, even to my ears, but I have the strangest feeling that my parents and I are prisoners in our home. That the man who they wanted me to get to know isn't who he says. He claims he's a pastor's son. I'm not convinced that's the truth."

"Anything else?" Nora asked. "I have a good memory. I'll relay anything you tell me."

Pressing her lips together, Mirabelle thought for a moment. "He acts strangely. He asks a lot of questions, and walks past the bank a lot, and then over to a stream. Today, a man came up and talked to him at it. He looked like a man on a Wanted poster that Tom had ripped down."

She took a deep breath and continued, "When I questioned him about how the man asked when I was going to cook for them, he got angry. That's when he struck me and told me to be quiet. Not to tell anything I'd overheard. I was hurrying home, but he caught up just as you spotted me."

"That man sets the hairs on the back of my neck standing straight," Nora murmured. "I don't like him." She sat back in her chair. "I'll pass what you've said along to Billy. Chances are, he might already suspect the man of something, and is investigating him right now."

"I sure hope so," Mirabelle said. "I am worried about my parents." Tears pricked at her eyes, but she refused to let them fall.

"I understand," Nora said. She reached over and squeezed Mirabelle's hand. "That man is still outside, pacing. I don't think we have long before he comes inside."

"It's all right. I've been able to tell someone," Mirabelle said, feeling the crushing weight of fear leave her. She stood. "If I leave, perhaps he'll think nothing of it."

"I hope you are right," Nora answered. "I'll stay. Give you time to leave, then I'll find my brother and tell him all you've said."

"Thank you," Mirabelle said. "I hope we get to meet again one day."

Nora nodded. "I do as well. I am sad to be leaving town so soon, but I'll be back, and I have the feeling we will be good friends." She smiled then. "Perhaps even family one day."

Mirabelle didn't know how to answer that, and simply smiled. She turned toward the door, and Tom had pulled it open the second she stepped out.

"What was that about?" he growled.

Mirabelle shook her head, and whispered loudly, "Her parents are going to be right upset when they find out. I don't dare speak of her situation here." Reaching for his arm, she gently rested a hand on it and said, "Being a pastor's daughter, gossip is unseemly. I'm sure you understand. You must have also had such strict rules growing up."

Tom hesitated, then nodded. "Yes. Of course. It...wasn't easy."

With a long sigh, Mirabelle nodded, and started walking toward her home. "Yes. I fully understand." She started to chatter about skirt lengths and sprained ankles and hid her smile as his eyes glazed over.

Fortunately, Tom said nothing else on the walk back. Mirabelle chanced a look behind her and saw Nora. The other woman gave a slow nod, and Mirabelle felt relieved. At least someone now knew there was something strange going on. She didn't feel so alone anymore.

The thought that Billy also wanted to bid on her lunch basket made her heart quicken. She wasn't going to lie to herself. It wasn't just that she wanted to share lunch with him and tell him her suspicions. She wanted to spend time with him. What would it be like, walking through the town with Billy holding her arm, not Tom?

Mirabelle was sure she'd feel comfortable. Relaxed. Happy. Not tense, worried, and strained. It was true, she didn't know much about love or men, but she knew, without a doubt, Tom was not the sort of person she could love.

Billy, though. She could imagine herself easily on his arm, walking through town with him, sitting and feeding the ducks in the small pond near the church, reading beside him on lazy afternoons, cooking for him. Those thoughts warmed her, and filled her with happiness. Not fear, like when she thought of Tom.

Why, if Billy tried to kiss her, she was sure it would be much, much nicer than when Tom had.

They approached the church, and her home beyond. Mirabelle's mother opened the door. Was that a flash of relief that went across her face as they entered? Mirabelle wanted to ask as her mother reached for her hand, but as usual, Tom followed them around.

There was no doubt in her mind now. Tom was up to something, and her mother suspected it as well. Mirabelle hung up her hat and handbag, and said a quick prayer that Nora would tell Billy all she'd said. It was obvious her family was going to need all the help they could get.

Chapter 15

Billy set down his fork. He had no appetite. Worry consumed him, and if he'd been at home right now, he'd have been pacing. Instead, he was at the hotel restaurant for a last meal with his sister before she left.

In a low voice, Nora had told Billy and Gavin, who had joined him, what had happened when she saw Mirabelle the prior day while he and Eli had been trying to learn more about the gang of robbers.

Billy's hand had clenched into a fist when Nora told him about the absolute terror in Mirabelle's eyes and how Tom had struck her. He wanted nothing more right now than to run to her house, break down the door, and comfort her.

He relaxed, though, when Nora told him how she'd quickly grabbed Mirabelle and led her to safety, but as she recounted the conversation they'd had, he grew tense again.

It was obvious Gavin was also concerned. He asked Nora to repeat Tom's description, and had asked pointed questions about his appearance, trying to get each detail from her as he hadn't seen Tom himself. With him being the acting sheriff, Gavin could—and would—act, but he was also now bound by the law, whereas Billy wasn't. And didn't plan to let anything get between him and Mirabelle's safety.

Nora now looked between the two of them. "I wish I didn't have to leave now. I want to stay and help you, and help Mirabelle. She seems like a sweet girl, Billy. No wonder you like her."

"You are welcome back at any point, sis. I mean it." Billy shook his head. "I won't lie. I'm going to miss you when you go." He pointedly ignored her comment about liking Mirabelle.

"It's a nice town," Nora said. "I'll be back. I promise you that. But what will you do about Mirabelle, and this so-called pastor's son? It's obvious you don't think he is one."

"No, I don't." He drummed his fingers on the table. "I only have a guess right now, and that's he's the leader of a gang. One going around robbing banks and post offices. If it's him, and it sure sounds it from the description, this wouldn't be the first time he'd pretended to be a pastor. Or

I guess, in this case, a pastor's son." Billy shook his head. "Part I don't get, though, is how Pastor Blackstone doesn't know."

"Mirabelle said there had been a letter from a man her father knew saying he was his son," Nora said. She shrugged. "Her father must believe the letter."

"He might. Being a man of the church, he tries to see the good in everyone, I suspect. Even if he has doubts." Billy sighed and picked up his fork, stabbing at the slab of cherry pie.

"What concerns me," Gavin said, looking around and then leaning in close, "is where are the rest of his men? Mirabelle saw one, that's obvious, but where are they hiding? Have they been walking through the town and no one's noticed them? I'm going to send a few men out to ride around the area, see what they spot. Abandoned homes or barns would be a good place to hide."

"Another good question," Billy said. "We'll need to watch closer. Not let the town go without one of us here keeping an eye out on things."

Gavin nodded. "I agree. We'll let Eli know. Together, we'll make sure someone is in town at all times."

"One of us, and a man who can ride out to get the others," Billy said.

"I'll find someone," Gavin said. "I may deputize a few." He stood up then. "Nora, have a safe trip. Billy, I'll find you later."

He walked away, and Billy took a long look at Nora. "I can't thank you enough for helping her," he finally said.

Nora reached across the table and squeezed his hand. "You're my brother. I'd do anything for you. I also sure couldn't leave her alone like that." She gave him a considering look. "Billy, what are you going to do? That man is no good."

"I know that," he answered, his jaw clenched. "Wish her father did. I don't know why he hasn't gotten rid of the man."

Alarm flashed over Nora's face. "I just remembered. She said she felt like they were prisoners, but her parents didn't seem to know. I wonder if they do. If maybe they've been threatened, and it's Mirabelle who doesn't know that. It's possible her parents have traded their lives for her protection."

"That'd be even worse," Billy said. "They're a good family. Even if the pastor and I don't see eye to eye on who Mirabelle should be courting with, that doesn't mean I'd wish them hard times."

His sister smiled at him then. "I think she likes you," she said. "Perhaps when this is over, things will be different between you and her father."

Billy's heart sped up. This time it wasn't from anger or nerves. "You think so?" he asked.

He wanted to hope that she was right. He knew there was a very real chance that he and Mirabelle might not ever be anything. They might not like each other once they got to be together, but they also might. And that possibility meant the world to him. It was what he wanted. What he longed for.

Just a chance.

"I know so. I told her you like fried chicken." Nora squeezed his hand again, sighed, and stood. She gave him a sad look. "It's time. I've got to go."

"I'll walk you," Billy said. He reached next to the table and grabbed Nora's bag. They walked to the stage station, where he handed up her bag to the driver, then hugged her tightly. "Safe travels," Billy said. "Give Ma my love."

"I will. Thank you for having me. Take care of yourself, won't you? And Mirabelle too," Nora said. She climbed inside the stage, then called to him, "You'd better write! Tell me what happens!"

The driver cracked the whip, and the stage drove off in a hurry of dust. Billy waved his hand in farewell. He waited until he couldn't see the stage, then slowly walked past the church.

The doors were closed, which was odd. The church was always open. That's how it was. A building for anyone at any time. He took up a position across the street, leaning against the side of a building, and pretended to read a newspaper he'd bought at the hotel.

This was a waiting game. The gang hadn't done anything yet. But he knew it was only a matter of time.

He'd be ready when they did. Mirabelle's life might depend on it.

Chapter 16

Mirabelle carefully wrapped the fried chicken and placed it in her basket, along with a jar of pickles, some bread slices, jam, and cookies. She glanced around the kitchen. What else should she add?

"Here," her mother said, coming over with a bowl. "I made potato salad."

"Thank you, Mama."

Mirabelle scooped half into a jar, then placed the jar into her basket and added forks and napkins. She hoped Billy would be there and place a bid on her lunch. She knew Tom thought no one would bid on her basket with him around. That honestly might be the case, and it worried her, even though Nora had assured her Billy planned to be there.

Tom and her father were in the room just beyond, ready to escort Mirabelle and her mother to the luncheon auction. Her body tense and heavy, Mirabelle sighed. She was tired. She couldn't remember the last time she'd slept well. Their home was filled with tension, all because of their unwanted guest. Who stood there in the doorway frowning. There was no way to delay further. It was time to go.

Her mother had packed her own basket. Of course, Papa would bid on it. He always did. The kitchen smelled wonderful right now. If only she had an appetite. At any other point, her mouth would be watering and her stomach growling.

As Mirabelle started to lift the basket, her mother moved closer, her voice low and her tone urgent. "Mirabelle. Something isn't right. I don't know what's happening. If you can get word to—"

"Ready?" Tom strode into the kitchen, his boots sounding heavily on the wooden floor. He didn't walk, ever. He stomped. "I don't understand why we have to go to this silly thing and we can't have our lunch right now. Here."

"It's for the charity fund," Mirabelle said, hoping he hadn't overheard her or her mother. "Papa must go. It's his fund. As the pastor's family, we must also go, and provide baskets. Did your family also do this back home?"

Her mother had moved silently to her father's side, holding her own lunch basket. She gripped it with both hands so tightly, her knuckles were white.

What had her mother been about to say? Get word to who? This must mean that her mother knew something was going on with Tom. The thought reassured her slightly.

"Charity starts in the home," Tom said. "I'm hungry now."

The last few days he'd been coarse, not even bothering to hide it. He made comments that weren't kind, almost as though he'd given up any pretense of being a decent individual.

"Perhaps you'll win a basket, then," Mirabelle said, offering him a faint smile.

"Who'd bid against me?" Tom bragged as he led the way.

It was a short walk. The church was practically in their yard, and the lawn was already filled with people. Mirabelle joined the women off to one side, holding her basket. The mayor stood before the crowd, making jokes and laughing. Almost everyone was smiling. The only ones who were not were her family. This was a social event that everyone looked forward to.

The men gathered around, and Mirabelle shivered. Tom was scowling right at her. He wasn't even pretending to be happy. Her eyes scanned the sea of faces, but she couldn't find Billy. Her heart sank just a little. He hadn't come. Had his sister been wrong?

"Let's start!" the mayor called. "You all know how this works," he said. "Cash only, and all the proceeds go to the town charity fund. Gentlemen bidders only; highest bid on a basket wins. Those who don't win a basket, well, the bakery has provided an assortment of muffins and savory rolls. Now," he added, looking around at the men, "don't be too nice. Outbid each other! It's for charity!"

There was laughter, and even Mirabelle couldn't help but smile. It was true. Not everyone wanted to outbid another, even if it was for charity. They were just too polite.

The bidding started, and before long it was Mirabelle's turn to stand before the crowd. She smiled as she held up her basket.

"Freshly made fried chicken." The mayor shook his head as he peered into her basket. "This looks mighty good."

"A dollar," Tom said.

There was silence. Mirabelle bit her lip. Wouldn't anyone bid against him?

"Five dollars," a voice called from the back. "I like fried chicken."

Mirabelle's head shot in that direction. It was Billy. Her heart started fluttering in excitement.

Or fear.

Right now, she felt both, and wasn't sure which was the most prominent of the two emotions.

Tom crossed his arms. "Ten dollars."

"Fifty." There were gasps, and Billy shrugged. "It's for the charity fund."

"You don't got fifty dollars," Tom growled.

"I've got more than that," Billy said, stepping closer. He reached into his pocket. "Fifty. Right here." He smirked at Tom. "I want chicken for my lunch today." He dipped his hand into his pocket again. "You know, let's make it an even hundred." He held the money out.

"My goodness," the mayor stammered. "My wife will want that hundred-dollar recipe, Missus and Miss Blackstone."

There was laughter rippling through the crowd. Mirabelle didn't know what to think. Tom's face was three shades past angry, and Billy looked amused. Her father looked...scared. Mirabelle glanced at her mother. She, along with most everyone else, was watching, eyes wide open and jaw slightly hanging. Mirabelle felt that way herself, honestly. Shock had her frozen to the spot.

"Fine. I'll take Mrs. Blackstone's basket," Tom said. "For a dollar." He rested a hand at his belt. "Unless someone's stupid enough to bid against me?"

No one answered, but there were surprised looks traded at his rudeness. Mirabelle watched as Billy strode up to the mayor, gave him the hundred dollars, and took the basket from her. "Let's find a spot," he said cheerfully, as though nothing unusual had happened.

Silently, Mirabelle followed, aware that Tom and her mother were close behind.

"Here's a good spot," Billy said, leading her to a shady spot against the church.

Mirabelle was pleased to see he'd been clever. The spot he chose had bushes on several sides with a bench in the middle, so it allowed for privacy. They could sit and be seen and talking, but not overheard if they kept their voices low. She nearly collapsed in relief.

A short distance away, she could see her mother setting out her own picnic, and Tom watching Mirabelle.

"Turn your back to him," Billy said.

"That might make him angry," Mirabelle gasped.

"He might also read lips," Billy said, one hand held over his mouth. "Turn your back so he can't see what you are telling me."

Mirabelle's eyes widened. "I'd have never thought of that," she whispered. "You are incredibly clever."

"Can't stay alive long as a gunslinger without having some smarts and some luck," Billy said. "So, excuse me in advance when I talk behind my napkin or behind my drink as I hide my own lips."

She nodded. "You chose a good place too," Mirabelle remarked, motioning around them.

"Yep. Scouted the place before the auction started. Gavin made sure no one else took it while I was bidding," Billy said. He reached into the basket and started pulling out the food.

"I got nervous when I didn't see you," Mirabelle said. She looked at him for a long moment. "I'm glad you are here. And that you bid on my basket."

"I want to spend time with you," Billy said, his face honest. Then he winked. "And if it upsets that false pastor's son in the process, well, so be it."

Mirabelle bit her lip. "So, you think he's lying about who he is?"

"I do." Billy helped himself to the chicken. "Nora told me she talked to you. What you said." He quickly repeated her story. "That's what she told me," he said. At her nod, he asked, "Has anything else happened? Or have you learned anything more?"

"Not other than how my parents seem to notice now. My father seems frightened. So does my mother. She tried to speak to me before we left. I think she wanted me to seek help, but she was interrupted, as Tom came into the room."

Mirabelle took a big breath. "He's everywhere. All the time. We are never alone. He's also started to slip in the way he acts. It's like he doesn't even try to pretend that he's nice anymore. You heard his comment about how no one had better outbid him on my mother's lunch basket.

He just sits around the house all day, making comments, eating, and watching us.

"He's been staying at the house at night too. Mama locks me in my room. I thought it was because he was there and she wanted to keep me safe, but last night, I heard him locking them into their room. We really are prisoners," she said, her voice catching.

"Is your father being blackmailed? Threatened? Can you think of any reason why this would happen?" Billy asked. Concern was all over his face.

She wasn't sure how to answer. "I don't know."

"That's okay. What about his friends? Do you know how many there are or where they are during the day? Has he let it slip?"

She shook her head. "No. I'm sorry."

"Don't be," Billy said. He took another bite. "He's watching us close," he said.

"I do know some of the places he's been," Mirabelle said. "Is that helpful?"

"It could be," Billy said. "Any information is better than none."

Grateful she might have some information to help, Mirabelle listed the places Tom had told her he'd been, as well as where he'd planned to go, and might take her. Billy listened carefully.

"I'll make inquiries," Billy told her with a frown. His eyes were serious, and she didn't doubt he took her seriously. "Especially if that's his next destination. My friends and I are planning to stop him before this goes much further. We've almost enough evidence to accuse him of the robberies that have been happening across the state. In the town where the last one took place, the leader of the gang matches his description. He'd pretended to be a pastor, then knocked out the sheriff."

With a gasp, Mirabelle looked at him.

Billy nodded somberly. "That's right."

Mirabelle looked down at her lap where her hands rested. They were trembling. She had never felt so frightened in her life. There was a shift in Billy's movement, and when she looked up, he had slid closer to her.

"Hey," he said softly, gently, as he looked her right in the eye. "Mirabelle, I'm going to take care of you. I'm going to protect you and your family. So don't worry. My friends and I are asking questions and keeping an eye on your house constantly. You don't see us, but we're there. I was there all morning, ready to protect you if I heard a scream. Tonight, it will be Eli. We aren't going to let anything happen to you. Now that I know he's there at night too, I'm more determined to put a stop to this—by whatever means necessary."

Even though she was scared, something about Billy's words filled her with comfort, and a small bit of peace fell over her soul. Mirabelle gave him a watery smile. "Oh, Billy," she said, "I'm so grateful for you."

They looked at each other for a long moment. Neither said anything, but so much hung between them. The air was filled with an electric current, and Mirabelle hoped it wouldn't ever go away. She could stay like this—feeling safe and wanted—for the rest of her life. She just wished it was under a different set of circumstances she was here with him.

"This is the part where I want to move closer and kiss you," Billy said softly.

That brought a genuine smile to her face. Billy reached over and held her hand. She longed to lean against him and let him wrap his arms around her. If only Tom weren't so near.

Mirabelle closed her eyes for a moment, and her racing heart slowed as his thumb stroked the back of her hand, relaxing her.

"This is where I'd let you," she whispered, as she looked up into his face.

Chapter 17

"Lunch is over. Mirabelle's mine again, rich boy," Tom snarled.

Mirabelle stiffened, but Billy simply nodded and slowly pulled his hand away. "Of course," he said. "Wouldn't dream of intruding. She was just telling me how the two of you are getting married."

Tom's eyes flicked between them, and it appeared something inside him relaxed as his posture eased. "That's right," he agreed.

"My congratulations to you both," Billy said. He walked over to Mrs. Blackstone. As he passed her, he hoped she heard when he whispered, "I know."

Gavin was on the other side of the street. Billy gave the smallest of nods, and followed as Gavin slipped behind a building.

"It's not good," Billy said, the moment he faced his friend. "He's locking them in their rooms at night. However, Mirabelle was able to give me a list of places he said he's been, and where he's planning to go."

"You look into those," Gavin said. "I'll watch him. As the sheriff, that's my job." He frowned then. "I have to do this legally, like it or not."

Billy nodded. He knew his friend was right. He had to be the one to make inquiries, to leave. But he didn't want to. He didn't want to leave Mirabelle. "Gavin," he started. He stopped then, unsure how to ask all he wanted to say.

"I'll keep her safe," Gavin promised. He reached out and put his hand on Billy's shoulder. "But we've got two choices and maybe not a lot of time. Do this legal like and put him away and keep your reputation that of a good man, or seek vengeance to remove the problem." Gavin shook his head. "Right now, she's safe enough. There's no reason for the second one. If that changes, we'll adjust our plan. Until then, you need to find out what you can, as quickly as you can."

"You are right," Billy agreed. He clenched his jaw. "It's just hard. I guess I know a little of how Eli felt when Hannah was being threatened."

"And just like before, we're going to come through this," Gavin assured him. "We always do, and this time won't be any different."

"Right." Billy frowned and pushed his hat up. "I'll be at the post office, sending messages to each of those towns."

Billy walked away, his shoulders feeling tight. Leaving Mirabelle's side was the opposite of what he wanted to do. Gavin was right, though. He had to learn all he could.

One way or another, he was going to get to the bottom of this. And it was going to be sooner rather than later.

***

Billy impatiently tapped his fingers on the post office counter. He'd stopped by there twice a day for the last four days only to have received no replies to his earlier letters seeking information. Today, by the looks of the stack of envelopes the clerk was carrying toward him, they'd either be rewarded or disappointed in their quest.

He hoped it wouldn't be the latter.

Billy nodded his thanks and took the bundle to the bench outside. Eli was there waiting for him, and Gavin walked up a moment later. Each of them started opening the envelopes.

"So far, nothing," Gavin said, after the second one.

"Don't give up," Eli said. "There's something in one of these. I feel it."

Billy reached for another envelope, then accidentally knocked a second onto the ground. As he leaned over to pick it up, a strange feeling washed over him. He put the first letter back into the stack and opened the second.

What he read chilled him through. He read it twice more to make sure he wasn't seeing incorrectly.

"Boys," Billy said, his voice low. "This is it." He looked up from the letter and held it out silently.

Eli was the first to snatch it from his hands. Anger flashing on his face, he held it to Gavin, whose jaw clenched as he read the words on the page.

"I knew it," Billy hissed, and slapped his thigh. "Deep inside, I knew there was something about that man. It's not even the fact he lied about being a pastor's son. It's the fact," and he looked down to read from the letter, "every place he's been, there's been at least one robbery—or a robbery and a murder."

"We've got what we need," Gavin said, and rose. "I'll raise a posse."

"I'll send someone to tell Hannah I won't be home for a while," Eli said, setting off at a jog.

His heart hammering a single word, *Mirabelle, Mirabelle, Mirabelle,* Billy broke into a run toward the pastor's house.

He didn't have a plan. He didn't know what he was going to do when he got there, but he had to make sure Mirabelle was safe. If some harm had befallen her, all because he was too slow in acting...

Billy tried to calm his fearful thoughts. He knew he couldn't think that way. It was important to stay calm. Focused.

The church was ahead, and just beyond it the pastor's house. Windows were closed, curtains drawn. The sight made him run faster. Billy got to the door and pounded on it. For the first time ever, he prayed Tom would open it.

After he punched the man in the nose, he'd make sure Mirabelle was safe.

There was silence beyond. Now, worry filled him. Billy raised his fist and knocked again.

If no one was answering, that was even worse. It might mean Tom had done something to the family. Billy stepped back, about to ram his shoulder into the lock, when the door opened.

Pastor Blackstone stood there, the fear apparent on his face.

"Mirabelle," Billy said. "Where is she?"

"She—she—I've—" The pastor was stammering so badly he couldn't stop. His whole body was trembling.

Billy grabbed hold of his shoulders and shook him. "Where is she?" he repeated.

From beyond, a figure drew closer, and Billy had his gun in his hand and pointed at the person before he could blink. A feminine scream made him lower it. "Mrs.

Blackstone," he said, pushing his way past the frozen pastor. "Where's Mirabelle?"

"He took her," she wailed, her voice near a scream. "He took my daughter!"

Her anguish was obvious, and it filled Billy with an ache. "Tell me everything," he said,. And then fixed his hardest glare on the pastor, "Everything. And then pray it's not too late for me to fix this mess."

Pastor Blackstone nodded, his Adam's apple bobbing as he whispered, "Of course, of course."

Billy moved further into the house and waited for the door to close. One finger to his lips, and the gun still in his hand, he asked, "Is there anyone else here?"

"No," Mrs. Blackstone answered, dabbing at her eyes with a handkerchief. "He left about ten minutes ago. Horace was just about to go get you."

"I was. I didn't know. You have to believe me," Pastor Blackstone said. Billy wasn't sure if that was directed toward him or to his wife. "Not at first," he continued. "I really thought he was the son of another pastor. The letter looked so real."

"He really had us fooled," Mrs. Blackstone said in a sob. "But after a few days, when he started acting differently, we began to wonder."

"Then I caught him," Pastor Blackstone said, nervously squeezing his hands together. "There was another man outside, and I overheard him talking. I wasn't trying to eavesdrop, but he asked when they were going to rob the bank. I must have made a noise, for Tom saw me, and that's when he threatened me."

"Threatened how?" Billy asked.

"He said he'd hurt Martha and Mirabelle if I didn't keep quiet," the pastor admitted. He looked at his wife. "I wanted to protect you both."

Mrs. Blackstone shook her head. "I know you did. But now, Mirabelle..." She broke into tears again.

"Do you know where they took her?" Billy asked impatiently. Time was wasting. Every minute she was gone was one she got further away.

"I don't," Pastor Blackstone said. "I must make amends. But I don't know how." He looked around the room in a panic. "I don't know what to do."

Billy met his gaze square on. "I do. I'm going to get Mirabelle back."

Chapter 18

"When's the grub gonna be ready?"

Mirabelle shrank back from the man leaning overtop of her, staring into the pot hanging above the small fireplace.

He moved away without waiting for an answer and joined Tom and two other men at a small table in the filthy kitchen.

As she stirred the stew—which Mirabelle hoped would be passable, due to the lack of ingredients available—she wondered how long it had been since Tom had kidnapped her. The sun had lowered some, leading her to think that though it felt like a long time had passed, it was likely only about two hours. Maybe three.

She knew the why. He wanted a cook. He also wanted someone who no one would suspect was his accomplice. The very idea of being forced to aid him in taking advantage of others made her feel sick to her stomach. The putrid smell from the oversized pot wasn't helping. Mirabelle had been greeted with the demand to finish cooking it the moment Tom had pushed her through the door.

The stew consisted of some rabbit, some half-rotted potatoes, wizened carrots, and a handful of mushrooms one of the men had gathered. She hadn't recognized the mushrooms the man had pointed out, so planned not to eat a bite. She'd rather go hungry if it came to it. If they were poisonous, she didn't want to be taken sick and suffer any more than she was. And if they were, perhaps she could take advantage and escape.

"What's my role?" one of the men asked.

Mirabelle pricked her ears. If she could find a way to warn the town these men were about to rob them, she would. Any detail might come in handy. She might be here as a prisoner, but she couldn't give up. Her mind was sharp, and she was sure she'd figure out something.

At least, she hoped she would.

"With the horses, Stan. Same as always," Tom said. "You're too stupid for anything else."

"Okay," Stan said.

"You'll be the front man again?" another man asked. "Being on account as you're the leader?"

"That's right," Tom said. "You'll just keep your gun close, Jimmy. Shoot anyone who moves."

The man, Jimmy, she supposed, pulled his gun out of his belt and fired it. Mirabelle screamed and dropped to the ground.

"Don't waste your ammo," was all Tom said, as he shot a glance her way.

Her hands shaking, Mirabelle picked up the ladle she was using and stirred the pot again for something to do to look busy, as much as to try and release some of her nervous energy. What kind of men were these? Firing a gun inside of a house?

Though this wasn't really a house. It used to be one, but it was obvious to her that the place had been abandoned for some time. It was about a twenty-minute ride out of town, if she'd estimated correctly. It had been hard to tell, facedown and jostled over a horse. Tom hadn't even allowed her the dignity of riding in the saddle.

The building was made up of four rooms. The kitchen and dining area, a sitting room, and two bedrooms. Mirabelle supposed that it didn't really matter what the place was like. As soon as the men had robbed the bank, they'd be leaving. Tom was saying so now.

"...then we ride to a few towns over, and keep quiet for a while." Tom looked up then and frowned at her. "That food ready yet?"

"Almost," Mirabelle said. She looked around for bowls, opening the cupboards. It didn't appear that there were any. There were some battered mugs and small spoons.

They would have to do. She ladled the stew into the mugs and carried them over to the table, then stepped back. She'd learned to do that quickly, or else one of the men would grab at her.

"What about her?" Stan asked. "Where's she gonna be during the heist?"

Tom frowned. Finally, he said, "I guess we'll get her on the way back through."

Mirabelle felt a tiny bit of hope form. If they left her here, perhaps she could escape. There must have been something in her eyes that shared that hope, because Tom added, "She'll be tied up and gagged." He smirked then. "No chance of warning the rich boy we're taking his money from the bank."

"But then we risk getting caught," Stan said, his voice a whine. "We got to come back for her, then go back, passing by that town. That's not a good idea, Tom."

He stopped talking when Tom glared at him.

"You don't tell me what to do," Tom said, his voice low.

"I'm glad we're leaving. I'm sick of this place," the fourth man said, who had been quiet until now. He was the one who she'd seen at the creek that day. "I'm ready to move on. These small towns never have much. Waste of time, if you ask me."

"But they're safer," Tom said, turning back to his food. "You know that, Charlie. Besides, I wasn't asking you. I'm the leader, remember?"

Charlie. Stan. Jimmy. Tom. Mirabelle repeated the names to herself. She didn't have much else, information wise, not even their last names, but she'd remember all she could. If they did take her to another town, perhaps she could pass their names and descriptions along to a sheriff. If she could escape.

Mirabelle tried to stifle the fear rising up in her. Right now, she'd give anything to be back with her parents. Back with Billy. But if her being here kept them safe until she found a way out, then that's what had to happen.

"More," Jimmy said, holding up his mug and waving his gun.

Quietly, Mirabelle refilled their stew. So far, none of the men seemed sick. Whether that was due to an iron stomach or luck, she couldn't say. It wouldn't be right to wish anyone ill, but she really did hope the mushrooms hadn't been of the safe variety.

"I still say you're making a mistake," Charlie said. His voice was low, and he hunched over his mug, spooning stew in his mouth.

"And why is that?" Tom asked.

"Because I heard there's gunslingers in town," Charlie said. "Eli Jones, Gavin Jefferson, and Billy Madison."

"Who are they?" Tom sneered. "Those names mean nothing to me. What, old men who've settled down for their final days?"

Charlie shook his head. "Nope. They aren't old. They're still top of their game. I heard tell they protect this town."

Tom snorted. "If that's true, then I wouldn't have her, now would I?" he asked, jerking his thumb toward Mirabelle. "They didn't do a good job protecting her."

He was quiet a moment, and the only sound that filled the air was the slurping of stew and the scraping of spoons. "You know," Tom said suddenly. "You might be right."

Charlie looked up.

"Not you. Stan." Tom pointed his spoon at the other man. "We run the risk of getting caught if we don't take her with us. So, tell you what, whoever wants her gets her." He pointed to Mirabelle again. "You men can fight over her once we've cleaned out the town. Only thing is we've got to watch out. If those gunslingers get word, maybe they'll want to try and prove how good they used to be."

Jimmy laughed, "I bet they are soft and out of shape. Not been in the game for a while." He sneered, "We'll take 'em out easy if they try and bother us."

Mirabelle opened her mouth to argue in the defense of Billy, Gavin, and Eli, then just as quickly closed it. She didn't want them to be expecting anything. Let them think the gunslingers were out of practice. Old, weak. Then, if they were caught off guard, things might go better for the town. If these men learned that she knew Billy, things could be much worse for her. Or him.

She let her eyes roam around the house. She had to escape. There was no way she was going to belong to any of these men. She walked to the table and took their dishes, returning to the small washbasin. As she knelt down to wash the dishes in the pail of water, she caught sight of a small, rusty kitchen knife that had fallen on the floor.

It wasn't much, and it wasn't large, but it was a weapon. Mirabelle wrapped it into a crusty rag also lying on the ground and slipped it into her pocket. Though it might not be much of a help, its weight made her feel better. She wasn't completely helpless now.

The men settled who was on watch. Stan won. The sun was setting, and exhaustion filled her. Mirabelle wondered, as she slumped in the corner of the kitchen, leaning her head back against the wall and pretending to rest, if she could slip out when he fell asleep. The way Stan's head was drooping gave her hope as she peered at him beneath her lashes.

The sound of heavy footsteps startled her. Stan too, by the way he jerked upright. Tom stood, watching him in disgust. "I knew you'd fall asleep," he said. Then he looked at Mirabelle. "And I knew you'd try to run when he did. I saw your eyes watching the door earlier." He pointed to one of the kitchen chairs. "Sit."

Trembling, Mirabelle stood and walked to the chair he indicated. When she sat, Tom pulled her arms behind her and secured them with a length of rope. Feeling panicked,

Mirabelle tugged against the rope. "Please! I won't try to run. Don't tie me up."

Tom knotted the rope tighter. "I know you won't. You can't move." He sat at the table with her, hunched over a map.

Tears filled Mirabelle's eyes. From the pain of the ropes digging into her arms or from her fear or anger, she wasn't sure. She just knew they were there. She closed her eyes, and the tears released.

If only Billy were here. But did he even know she was kidnapped?

Chapter 19

Billy was about out of patience. Mirabelle needed him, and he wasn't getting many answers from her parents. It was time to go and see who else could help. He threw open the front door. To his relief, Eli and Gavin were just a few feet away.

"Mirabelle's been kidnapped," Billy said. "I don't know where she's at. But it sounds like they're planning to hit the bank soon. So they can't be far."

"I've got men gathering now," Gavin said, always calm. Billy was grateful for that. Right now, he was anything but. Usually, it would be him with a joke to lighten the mood. Right now, all he wanted was to tamp down the worry coursing through him.

"We'll find her, Pastor Blackstone," Eli promised. "We won't come back without her."

"We had no idea. You must believe us," Mirabelle's mother said. She grabbed Billy's arm. "Say you believe me! I'd never put my darling girl at risk."

Billy took her hands in his and squeezed them gently. "I know that. And I also know that Mirabelle loves you. She won't blame you either."

Mrs. Blackstone shocked him then. She turned to her husband and put her hands on her hips. "You are going to do right by Mirabelle, and let her court with Billy if she wants. You owe that to her, and much more."

The pastor's eyes widened as his wife continued, now shaking her finger at him. "And furthermore, I will be in control of hem heights, not you. If I want to take my skirts up a half inch, that's just what I'll do."

Her voice was shrill, and Billy felt confused about the last part. He glanced at Eli and Gavin, who also looked puzzled.

"I agree, I agree," the pastor said, holding up his hands. "I just want my daughter back." He turned then to Billy. "But I'm coming with you. My daughter needs me, and I won't let her down."

Billy nodded. "You got a horse?"

The pastor hesitated. "Ah. No."

That wasn't too much of a surprise. Living in town, the man likely didn't have need for one, and could rent from the livery when he had to go to the outskirts to visit folks.

There was a long pause, and Billy looked up as Eli cleared his throat. "Pastor, forgive me the question, but time is of the essence. You can ride a horse, can't you?"

There was a heavy silence. Billy's eyebrows shot up, and Gavin's jaw dropped. Finally, Mrs. Blackstone answered, "He can't. Horace is terrified of the things."

Pastor Blackstone straightened his shoulders. "Martha, please." He turned to Eli. "I'll do what I must to help my daughter. Get me on it and point me toward where I need to go, and with the Lord's guidance I'll get there."

Billy turned and left. He wasn't sure what to think, and he wasn't about to say a thing, seeing as Mrs. Blackstone had suggested that he and Mirabelle might start courting. There was no way he was going to ruin his chances by making light of the pastor's situation.

Thankfully, Eli had things well under control. He could hear him assuring the pastor he'd look out for him.

Gonna have to eat a lot of Meg's cookies as a thank you to him. Maybe even in front of her. He shuddered. But anything for Mirabelle.

Gavin followed him and started calling instructions to several men who had clustered nearby. Billy mounted and listened as Gavin split the three of them up, each with three additional men. The pastor rode up, clinging for dear life to an old gray mare. He had a panicked look in his eyes as he leaned forward, hugging the horse around her neck.

"Loosen a bit," Billy said, riding close. "Else you'll choke her. Maybe even fall off."

The mare was old and tame, often used to teach children to ride, so she was a good choice. He met Eli's eyes, and they traded grins, choosing to find the humor in the tense situation. It was that very thing that kept them going at times like these. You never knew what was going to happen on a manhunt with a hostage.

"They can't be too far away," Gavin said. "Marcus says there's an old shack east, about fifteen or so minutes' hard ride. That's the most likely spot. You want to try that first? We'll come at different angles."

Billy nodded. "Sounds good to me. Anyone have other ideas?"

Shaking his head, Gavin said, "They all agree, that's the best one. It's been abandoned for a while. Seeing as we are newer to town, I'm thinking they know the area best."

"I agree." Billy started in the direction. "I'll approach the front."

"Rear," Eli called.

"I'll be standby," Gavin said.

Standby meant he'd hang back just a little, to see which of his friends needed reinforcement. If Tom and his gang were in that shack, and they went out one door or the other, they'd be met with a force of men larger than theirs. Odds were in their favor today. But the sun was starting to set, and Billy was getting worried. If they were wrong, and Mirabelle wasn't being held there, they were losing valuable time.

There was also the possibility that the men were watching, planning to rob the bank while the posse was out searching for them.

"Wait!" the pastor called, still clinging, though slightly less, to his horse.

Everyone stopped and looked at him. As best as he could, the pastor straightened up. "We should pray," he said. When the men nodded and bowed their heads, Pastor Blackstone said, "Lord, we ask you to help us find Mirabelle, to bring those who would do her and our town harm to justice, and to protect us each. Amen."

At the chorus of amens, the men started to ride. Billy pulled in the lead. He wasn't planning to slow until he was close enough to see the speck of the building. Mirabelle was depending on him.

Whoever had given the information was right. They were there in around fifteen minutes. The men slowed and split, coming in at an angle. Billy and his group slipped off their horses, and slowly approached the shack. He'd told Pastor Blackstone to wait with the horses.

Quietly, they creeped close. It was twilight now. Inside, someone lit a lantern, and Billy took the opportunity to count. He saw four men. But where was Mirabelle?

Just then, he heard a woman's cry. "Stop!"

The pastor heard it too and started running toward the shack. "Mirabelle!" he shouted.

His desperate attempt to get to his daughter gave them away, and there was a gunshot, whizzing right past Billy's hat.

Chapter 20

When Tom had tried to kiss her, Mirabelle had twisted away as best as she could and screamed. What she didn't expect was to hear her father shouting her name.

Faster than she could blink, Jimmy had aimed and fired. Mirabelle struggled against her ropes. Had he shot her father? Someone else? Desperate, she tried to free herself.

Still tied to the chair, there wasn't much Mirabelle could do but twist and tug. Tom and his gang raced to different windows and started firing their guns. Mirabelle remembered the knife then. Somehow, she managed to twist enough to get the handle to brush against her fingertips. It was still too far away, though, for her to grab.

"You're surrounded, and the sheriff is here. Time to come out," she heard Billy call.

Mirabelle stifled her gasp. Billy was here! Redoubling her efforts to get free, she paused only when Tom turned to the others.

"We're going to cause a distraction," he said, voice so low she could hardly hear. "Then we'll escape. Get to the horses and go."

She was blinking, wondering what he was going to do, when Tom threw the lantern into the fireplace.

There was an explosion, and Mirabelle barely had time to lean forward and cover her face. Flames licked through the kitchen area, hungrily coming toward her. The heat was searing, and the flames devoured the dry wood of the house, filling it with smoke.

Cracking and popping filled her ears, and panic her body. She had to be calm. Had to focus on getting out. It wouldn't be long before the house was fully ablaze and there would be no escape.

She began to cough. The smoke made her lungs ache, and her eyes watered fiercely. It was so difficult to breathe, her head was starting to feel light. Smoke was growing thick and her eyes burned.

The knife finally reached her hands, and then fell to the ground. "No!" she cried in frustration. "No!"

Mirabelle tried to stand, to shuffle or move away from the fire. It was closer now. The heat was intense, and her hair clung to her face and neck. Was this how it was all going to end? Burned in a fire? Tom and his gang had fled, and left her to die alone.

Would her parents ever know that she loved them? Would Billy? He was here, somewhere, but was he hurt? A sob burst through Mirabelle, and hopelessness filled her. She struggled again, a last, desperate attempt to save herself, but it was so hard to breathe. How long before the flames reached her? Would the smoke render her unconscious first?

There was a crash, and the door on the opposite side burst open. Through the smoke, Mirabelle could only faintly make out a figure. "Mirabelle! Mirabelle!"

It was Billy. He had come for her.

Or had he? Was this a dream? It didn't matter if it was. She'd answer him anyway. If she was to be burned inside the house, it was a tender mercy that her last thoughts might ease the pain.

"Over here!" Mirabelle coughed, choking as the smoke filled her throat and flames licked at the back of her chair.

Billy grabbed her, and Mirabelle nearly cried in relief that he was real. He pulled her to stand, or tried to, as he then saw she was bound. He pulled out a knife and cut loose the ropes that had dug into her, then held her closely in his arms as he carried her from the house and the fire consuming it.

As the first sweet breath of fresh air filled her lungs, Mirabelle was stunned to see the entire home ablaze. She hadn't realized it was entirely on fire. It had been a nearer miss than she'd imagined.

Fear filled her as it dawned on her how close she'd come to death. How close Billy had come. He'd risked his life to enter the blazing building and find her.

Billy set her down, then appraised her. "Are you hurt?" he asked, urgency in his voice as his eyes roamed over her.

"No. You saved me just in time." Mirabelle sagged against him in relief.

He wrapped his arms around her, and Mirabelle had never felt anything so wonderful. There was no time to say more before Billy helped her on his horse.

"Stay here. I have to make sure they got everyone," he said.

"There are three others besides Tom," Mirabelle said. "Jimmy, Stan, and Charlie."

He looked up at her and gave a solemn nod. "We won't let a single one get away. They'll pay for what they did to you and your family."

Shots rang out, and Billy ran toward them. Her father appeared then. Mirabelle looked at him, and felt surprise. He was crying. "Papa?"

"You're alive," he whispered as he reached for her. "My Mirabelle. I'm so sorry. Please forgive me. I'll explain everything later, but I never meant for harm to come to you. I was trying to prevent it. I swear."

She squeezed his hand. "I know, Papa. I love you."

There were shouts and several gunshots. Mirabelle flinched at each, and slid off the horse to cling to her father. His arms tightened around her. What was happening? Was someone hurt? Was it Billy?

Across the distance she could see a man running, and another tackle him. She couldn't see who was who. There were more gunshots, and Mirabelle didn't know where to look to find Billy. There was too much happening all at once, and the smoke and the flames made it more difficult to see. She clutched her father tighter.

"I feel like this is all my fault somehow," she said, looking up at him in fear. "If one of them gets hurt..."

"The fault is mine," her father said quietly. "But they are good men. Quick, clever, and the Lord is with them. I see that now. They were sent to protect our town and all who live in it."

Mirabelle could hardly breathe at her father's words. It sounded as though he would be welcoming now to the gunslingers. Hope filled her.

A figure, limping, but not pointing a gun at them walked out of the smoke. It was Billy. His shirt was torn, and there was black soot from the fire all over him, but he gave her that grin of his, and tipped his hat. "We've all of them. Time to take them back to town and put them in the jail. Pastor Blackstone, can you manage to ride again?"

Her father nodded. "Yes, of course. I just need a little assistance up."

Mirabelle watched, the hint of a smile trying to break free as she watched her father helped on an old gray horse. She knew how much he hated horses after one had bit him as a young man, early in his pastor days.

Billy returned a moment later and swung up effortlessly in front of her. Shyly, Mirabelle wrapped her arms around his middle.

"I'm so glad you came for me," she said quietly.

"I just wish I'd been here sooner. No, I wish it had never happened. I let you down by not protecting you." Billy's voice was low.

"That's not true," Mirabelle said. She rested her cheek against his back. "I hope now, Papa will let me get to know you better."

"I think he might." Billy's voice held a touch of amusement in it. "Your mother gave him quite a fussing. She also said something about hemlines."

"Hemlines?" Mirabelle brightened. "Well then, if this whole escapade both gets me a chance with you and a half inch higher on my skirts, I'm quite happy it happened." She laughed, surprising herself at how light she felt.

They were back to town before she knew it, and she was astonished at how many people were there. It was almost dark, and many held lanterns to provide light. Billy climbed down, then wrapped his arms around her waist and lowered her slowly. Mirabelle didn't step away.

Her mother came running over. "My baby!" she shrieked, and hugged Mirabelle. Then she hugged Billy. "My dear boy. You are welcome at any time in our home."

That was all Mirabelle needed to hear. She turned to Billy, and made sure her voice was loud enough to carry. "You not only saved me, but you and your friends saved our town. A hero deserves a reward."

Then, before anyone could even take a breath, she stood on her tiptoes and kissed Billy sweetly, fully on the lips. It was everything and better than she'd imagined it would be. Mirabelle hoped Billy felt the same.

When she pulled away a few seconds later, she was delighted to see his silly grin and bright red face faintly against her mother's lantern. Even the tips of his ears were pink.

Her father cleared his throat, and Mirabelle looked at him. "So, does that mean you'll be courting now?"

Mirabelle smiled at Billy. "Why, yes. Yes, it does."

Epilogue

Mirabelle tucked her hand into Billy's arm. They were slowly walking through town, looking in all the shop windows on the way back to her home after a lunch at the hotel restaurant. They passed by Callie, who giggled and waved at them before ducking into a store.

"Billy," she asked suddenly. "When we get married, will you invite Nora? I'd love to see her again. Of course, Callie must be there."

"I'll write to her today," Billy promised. He paused to kiss her hand, then they started walking again.

"It would be nice if she lived closer," Mirabelle sighed. "It's not just because she helped me, but I really like her. I want to be friends."

"You know, she mentioned something about coming back for a while. Maybe you can convince her to stay," Billy answered.

"That would be wonderful. I will do my best. Oh, look! Gavin's hanging out a sign," Mirabelle said.

They watched as Gavin straightened the sign that said: *Sheriff Gavin Jefferson.* He went back inside the sheriff's office, though he left the door open.

"He'll be a good sheriff," Billy commented as they walked closer. "He's not ready to hang up his hat yet, even if Eli and I are comfortable being part-time gunslingers."

"I'm glad," Mirabelle said. "You shouldn't ever give up something you love, not when it's a part of you."

Gavin caught her eye through the doorway and nodded at her. She smiled in return. It had been nice getting to know Gavin a little more. He was quiet, which surprised her. It was obvious that he was the thinker of the group.

She felt so welcomed into the circle of friends. Gavin had treated her as a sister, and so did Eli and Hannah. She'd never felt so accepted so quickly.

After courting for several months, Billy had asked her to marry him. He had bought fifty acres and was building a house. Originally, he and Gavin had planned to buy that land together, but both agreed that he should have it to build a new house on. He'd cleverly started construction in a spot where they'd see Gavin's house from their window.

She was looking forward to that. After all, Gavin might settle down himself one day, and then she'd have a female neighbor and friend right nearby. Until then, she and Billy could still have dinner with Gavin on the nights he was home, and help keep him company.

Her parents were delighted about the upcoming nuptials, and her mother had been planning food and decorations. They were supposed to sample cakes she'd made once they got back to the house.

Billy squeezed her hand as they drew closer to her home. She returned the gesture, her heart light. Mirabelle didn't know when she was last so happy.

Her mother waved to her from the door. "Look!" she said, twirling around. "My dress is returned from the dressmaker." She pointed at the hem. "A half inch higher. It makes all the difference."

"I can't wait for mine." Mirabelle smiled. "Callie was quite right to suggest it."

She and Billy walked into the kitchen. Her father was there, slicing several small cakes. He looked up at them. "Hello, you two."

"Papa," Mirabelle said, kissing his cheek. "Oh, that looks good. What cake is this?"

"This one has a raspberry filling," he said. Then, he pointed in turn to two others. "Peach, and buttercream."

"I don't know how we will choose," Billy said. He sat at the table and picked up a fork. "Mrs. Blackstone, nothing you make tastes bad. A man could grow heavy with your attention in the kitchen."

Mirabelle's mother blushed. "You are a dear thing," she said, patting his shoulder.

Her father pushed plates with a slice of each cake on it toward her, Billy, and her mother. "Sample! Tell us what you like best. I want my daughter to have whatever makes her happy."

"Oh, Papa, I have all I need," Mirabelle said. "I have you both, and I have Billy."

Her father cleared his throat. "I still feel regretful. Embarrassed that I was fooled, and by the time I discovered it, harm had been done."

Billy shook his head. "Pastor Blackstone, you did what you thought you had to do to protect your family. No one faults you for that. But next time, if you need us, any of us, myself, Gavin, or Eli, I want you to come to us right away. That's why we are here. To keep the people of Red Ridge safe."

Her father shook Billy's hand. "You're a good man. I'm proud my daughter has chosen you."

Mirabelle's mother sniffled, and dabbed at her eyes. "I'm just so happy," she said.

The smile that escaped was so enormous that Mirabelle could hardly hold it on her face. She'd also never felt so happy. Billy smiled at her and picked up his fork again.

She watched as he took bite after bite, laughing and talking easily with her parents.

Her father had been right, she suddenly realized as she heard him joke with Billy. A man can change. Only, it hadn't been Billy, but her father who had.

And she couldn't think of a better thing to have happened in all the world.

What's next?

Find out what happens when Gavin is determined to help
a woman out of a mess, and winds up in a situation he
might not be able to get out of.
Book 3: The Lawman
https://www.amazon.com/dp/B0DQ7HFQ15

***

And if you haven't already, be sure to get your FREE book
in the Red Ridge Chronicles right here:
https://dl.bookfunnel.com/dt01yp1w38

Note from Author

Thank you for taking the time to read *The Drifter*.
Could I ask for one small favor? Reviews like yours on
Amazon mean so much to me and help others to find my
books! Even just a single line means a lot!
Also...
Want a FREE book?
Stop by my website to get your no strings attached **FREE
book**. It's my gift to you, as a thank you for reading this
one.
www.sarahlambbooks.com

Want a Free Red Ridge Chronicles Prequel?

Enjoy the gunslingers' adventure that happens just before Eli answers Hannah's ad.

The Riders

When an old friend calls, legendary gunslingers Eli Jones, Billy Madison, and Gavin Jefferson answer without hesitation. They've faced down the toughest outlaws, always bringing justice with deadly precision and no remorse. But nothing could prepare them for the fiery Stella, a woman determined to blaze her own trail—even at risk to one of their own.

As they race to prevent a catastrophe, the trio soon realizes that love is a more dangerous adversary than any outlaw.

These quick-draw, sharp-witted gunslingers have always sworn off settling down, but what happens next might just change their minds.

Discover the electrifying prequel to the Red Ridge Chronicles, a historical romance series in ebook, paperback, large print, and audiobook.

Read it in ebook here:

https://dl.bookfunnel.com/dt01yp1w38

Listen to it in audiobook here:

https://dl.bookfunnel.com/bq8tiktnwu

Read or Listen to the Red Ridge Chronicles Books

Amazon: https://www.amazon.com/dp/B0DQ7HFQ15
Audible:
https://www.audible.com/author/Sarah-Lamb/B098H3
SGLK

Book 1

The Gunslinger

Book 2

The Drifter

Book 3

The Lawman

Book 4

The Doctor

Book 5

The Tracker

Book 6

The Newcomer

Book 7

The Old Man

Book 8

The Christmas Rescue

About the Author

Sarah writes captivating characters and clean romance that's anything BUT boring! From heartbreaking moments to heartwarming tales, get swept away in either historical or small town romance that pulls you in until the last page.

Nestled in the Blue Ridge Mountains of Virginia where she's married to her Texan husband, you'll find Sarah creating her next book, homeschooling her two boys, or volunteering in her community.

Want more of Sarah's books? Find them all on Amazon!

https://www.amazon.com/stores/Sarah-Lamb/auth
or/B098H3SGLK